Death Takes the Veil
and Other Stories

Death Takes the Veil
and Other Stories

Monica Quill

*With an introduction
by Ralph McInerny*

Five Star • Waterville, Maine

This collection is a work of fiction. Names, characters, places, and incidents are either the product of the author's imagination, or, if real, used fictitiously.

Five Star First Edition Mystery Series.

Published in 2001 in conjunction with Tekno-Books and Ed Gorman.

The text of this edition is unabridged.

Set in 11 pt. Plantin by Elena Picard.

Printed in the United States on permanent paper.

Library of Congress Cataloging-in-Publication Data

Quill, Monica, 1929–
     Death takes the veil and other stories / Monica Quill ; with an introduction by Ralph McInerny.
          p.cm.—(Five Star first edition mystery series)
          Contents: Death takes the veil—Intent to kill—Miss Butterfingers—The other urn—A rose is a rose is a rose—A sound investment—The visitor.
     ISBN 0-7862-3143-2 (hc : alk. paper)
     1. Detective and mystery stories, American.   I. Title.
II. Series.
PS3563.A31166 D35 2001
     813′.54—dc21   2001033052

For Theron Raines
With gratitude
And
For Rex Stout
In memoriam

Table of Contents

How I Took the Veil

Once my Father Dowling mystery series was established, Theron Raines, my agent at the time, suggested that I think of a series featuring nuns. Perhaps he was joking. But it had been at his suggestion that I turned to mysteries in the first place, so I was inclined to attend both to his words and to the penumbra of suggestion that might attach to them. In any case, the suggestion fascinated me.

For one thing, it was a dare. When I took part in NPR's Prufrock Murders a few years ago—a novel written by a series of different writers, each seeking to make the task more difficult for the writer of the next chapter—it was kind of a collective dare. At the end, I was asked to do the final chapter as well, which amounted to the challenge of finding a unified and more or less plausible finale for randomly assembled parts. I was particularly flattered to be asked to do that since it amounted to a vote of confidence in my technical abilities. And it was sort of "I double dare you." Irresistible.

However happenstance the occasion for writing something might seem, the writing itself is a serious matter. In responding to Raines' suggestion of a mystery series involving nuns, I set about it with the utmost seriousness. And of course within the constraints of the genre. For better or worse, Sherlock Holmes and Dr. Watson continue to haunt the mystery genre, especially when characters continue into other stories. You could make a study of successful mystery series and see if this is true. Somebody has probably already done it. When I went to work on what became my Sister Mary Teresa Dempsey series—Emtee Dempsey, as she is irreverently if affectionately called—I deliberately modeled it on Rex Stout's Nero Wolfe mysteries.

Stout produced Nero Wolfes over many decades, both novels and novellas, and seems never to have tired of writing them, or to hanker after other genres. Prior to writing mysteries, he had written turgid psychological dramas no one even remembers. Maybe at first he thought of writing mysteries as a kind of come down. But the Depression was on, and like everyone else he needed money. Many who have had the knack of writing popular fiction profess to be half ashamed of it and to consider themselves really meant for more exalted work. The man who became famous as Max Brand referred dismissively to his westerns and Dr. Kildare novels. In his own mind he was a poet, and after churning out his daily words, sometimes as many as 10,000 a day, he devoted himself to writing epic poems. Dreadful stuff. And of course Conan Doyle became almost a whiner about the popularity of Sherlock Holmes, having to resurrect him after the crime of killing him off. Stout, by sunny contrast, seemed never to have looked back once he had put his hand to the plow.

Archie Goodwin is the narrator of the Nero Wolfe mysteries. He works for and professes to be in awe of the great man, though it dawns on the reader that Archie does most of the work. Nero almost never leaves the Manhattan brownstone in which he is ensconced with chef, valet, gardener, hothouse on the roof, and of course Archie. Clients come to the door, and are accepted only with great reluctance by Nero who would prefer to read, sip beer and cultivate orchids. But money is needed to keep up the establishment, so, usually at Archie's insistence, the client is accepted. Soon there is a murder and Archie and a team of ad hoc assistants gather information for the great man to interpret. The stories end in Nero's study with police and suspects all around him. Despite all that we and the others in the room know, Nero alone comes up with the murderer.

How could one use such a model in a series about nuns? Emtee Dempsey, a septuagenarian nun, is my Nero Wolfe. She is ensconced in a house designed by Frank Lloyd Wright, given to the order by a benefactor, and one of only two pieces of property salvaged by the M&M's, the Order of Martha and Mary, when things spun out of control after Vatican II. The college the order ran is gone, the property sold, but women who studied history with Emtee Dempsey look her up in the house on Walton Street in downtown Chicago. And they bring with them the mystery to be solved. There are two young nuns in the house, Sister Joyce and Sister Kimberly. They do not wear the traditional habit, as the old nun does. Joyce cooks and keeps the house going; Kim is a graduate student at Northwestern, the research assistant for Emtee Dempsey who is at work on a history of the twelfth century, and more or less my Archie Goodwin. Also, she has a brother who is a detective in the Chicago police department, who provides a source of information not easily available to nuns. The stories culminate in the house on Walton Street, with Emtee Dempsey doing her Nero Wolfe imitation.

Only connoisseurs of mysteries will notice this inexact parallel. I mention it because it was crucial for me when I designed the series. With time, I stopped using a single viewpoint, that of Kimberly, and turned to multiple viewpoint, which I greatly prefer.

The initial suggestion that I write a mystery series was prompted by the fact that in several novels of mine priests featured prominently. My agent was reading the Rabbi Kemelman mysteries and had an epiphany. He called and somewhat excitedly told me his great idea. I should write a mystery series featuring a priest! My reaction was equivocal. I had no idea how to write a mystery. And I had a small reputation as a novelist I wished to cultivate. Would such a move be, perhaps, *infra dig?* But I was tempted and dealt with temptation in the Oscar Wilde way—I succumbed.

Rereading Rex Stout removed my fear of trying. It seemed to me that once there was a body on the floor, a Nero Wolfe mystery consisted of digging up a series of suspects and then eliminating them one by one. When there was none left, it fell to Nero Wolfe to see what no one else had seen, identify the killer and that was that. Did Rex Stout know when he began who did it? I doubted it. So I began with my cast of characters, got a body on the floor and then went in search, as I drafted the story, of plausible suspects and eventually the murderer to be identified by my sleuth. This insight, if that is what it was, had enabled me to launch the Father Dowling series, and it worked as well with the Monica Quills.

Monica Quill, i.e. pen name, was used because I had the same publisher for both series and this was meant to avoid any resistance to bringing out one of each every year. I have launched four other series since, only one under a pseudonym, and leave the logistics of publication to others. I write a non-mystery novel from time to time, but like Rex Stout I am happy as a lark to be writing mystery novels and to have a number of series, each of which has a sufficient number of fans to keep them, and me, going. I began the Andrew Brooms to get out of church, so to speak, wanting a series without nuns and priests, but not because I lost my zest for Father Dowling and Sister Mary Teresa. Being a priest or nun in imagination for the course of a novel is probably good for my soul. It hasn't hurt my income either. But even if the series were less successful than they are, I would continue to add to both.

This volume contains four novellas and is, in its way, a further sign of Rex Stout's influence on me. Stout published a Nero Wolfe mystery like clockwork every year. At the same time, he was publishing Nero Wolfe novellas, usually in *Cosmopolitan*. From time to time, not quite annually, he brought the novellas out in threes, the title of the volume ringing the changes on the number three. These Monica Quill novellas have appeared in magazines and now they are brought together in a single volume. Could anyone be surprised that I dedicate this volume to the memory of Rex Stout? And use the occasion to express my gratitude to Theron Raines?

Ralph McInerny

Death Takes the Veil

A Sister Mary Teresa Mystery

1

Sylvia Corrigan had been an actress in college, on stage, in the classroom, everywhere, until acting became indistinguishable from living. In interviews, she would go on about it, suggesting that the journalist posing the questions was also playing a role.

"I watch you," she would say, her famous green eyes narrowing, making a gesture that seemed fraught with significance, "and already I covet your role. I want to play it. How long have you been with *Newsweek*?"

And, as the abashed reporter later wrote, that quickly they had exchanged roles, Sylvia questioning, the reporter answering. Two days later the profile Sylvia had written arrived in the journalist's mail.

Such precocity—Sylvia called it genius, but considered genius a fate rather than an accomplishment—while at first eliciting amazement and praise, had a way of cloying quickly. One role Sylvia had never mastered was that of friend. A friend after all must be constant.

An alumna who was in films, informed of the young Sylvia's talent, had come to the college production of *The Lady's Not For Burning* and assured Sister Mary Teresa Dempsey that the student actress's future was assured. Emtee Dempsey had wondered even then if this were good luck or bad. She had wondered the same thing about the closing of the college. The property had been sold off, and only a remnant of the Order of Martha and Mary (the M&M's) remained, lodged in a wonderful house on Walden Street designed by Frank Lloyd Wright, gift of yet another grateful alumna. Former students kept in touch, bringing their troubles and triumphs to Emtee Dempsey and she came to relish the role of wise old friend. She was surprised, therefore, to be told by Joyce of Sylvia's appearance on *Kup's Show*.

"Sylvia is in Chicago?"

"She's going to play Medea. Only a short engagement because she's scheduled to make a film. An adaptation from a French writer. George Bananas?"

"Bernanos," Emtee Dempsey said. No error of fact ever went uncorrected in her presence.

"About some Carmelite Martyrs."

"A tremendous play!" Emtee Dempsey said. "Do you know it, Sister Kimberly? The Dialogues of the Carmelites."

Kim was the third of the trio of M&M's in residence on Walton Street, a graduate student in history at Northwestern but, more important—certainly it consumed more of her time—research assistant to Sister Mary Teresa, who was writing a massive history of the 12th century.

"No, I haven't."

"You'll find it on that shelf there." She rose a little behind the desk in her study. Unlike the younger women, Emtee Dempsey always wore the traditional habit of the order as decreed by the foundress, Blessed Abigail Keineswegs. The headdress gave the impression of a gull landing, the wimple was a large starched affair, the robe black, the cincture white. She had yet to hear a convincing argument why nuns should dress like other women. To remove barriers? Perhaps there should be barriers. In any case, Emtee Dempsey had never felt under any handicap wearing her eighteenth century garb. She was an internationally recognized medieval historian and the one teacher no student was ever likely to forget.

"You can read it aloud to me."

"In French?"

"It will be good practice." She added, in belated and not wholly sincere self-deprecation, "For my ear."

The old nun had little doubt that Sylvia Corrigan would visit Walton Street. She did whenever she came to Chicago. In that at least she was like other alumnae.

"Do we have that thing she drinks? White wine and . . ."

"Creme de Cassis," Joyce said. "It's called Kir."

"Not an ungrateful one, I hope. She may want to stay for dinner."

It turned out that Sylvia wanted a good deal more than that. She wanted to live with them.

Her telephone call came while Emtee Dempsey was still thinking of things Sylvia would want when she visited. Now she was able to ask their expected guest what they could do to make her visit more enjoyable. Emtee Dempsey would have indignantly denied that the prominence of her former students played any part in the fuss she made over them, but she seemed to follow Sylvia's career with unusual interest.

"Just a cell like any of yours," Sylvia said in rare tones. Her voice, like her manner, had the ability to assume different pitches, accents, pronunciations. It was hard to know what persona Sylvia had adapted. "I will live according to your schedule, go to chapel with you, everything. Is there a copy of the rule?"

"Why don't you simply take the veil, Sylvia?"

"That is precisely what I shall be doing."

A nun for the nonce, that is. Sylvia could adopt, as an actress, an indefinite number of lifetime commitments. But in real life the only role she could no longer play was that of Sylvia Corrigan.

"I am a blank piece of paper. A role has to be written on me."

She had never married. There were equivocal references to her liaison with Carlos Bonifacio, an Argentine whose career flourished in both North and Latin America. He would be appearing with her in the film adaptation of Bernanos' play.

"I want to be a nun," Sylvia said.

Being a nun was not as definite a thing as it once had been. Bernanos' Carmelites would recognize the Carmelites of today, but such minor orders as that founded by Abigail Keineswegs had undergone profound upheavals and faced total extinction. But Sylvia's impression of the M&M's would have been formed at college and even so short a time ago as that they had been numerous, disciplined, distinctive. Sylvia's motive in inviting herself, given these changes, led to predictable difficulties when Sylvia arrived.

On previous occasions she had been brought to the door in a limousine and so quickly did her entourage produce a crowd that her passage from car to door was a royal one, as she threw kisses to her fans, touched an outstretched hand here and there, refused autographs. On this visit, when Kim went to the door she found a waif. Hair pulled back in a ponytail, wearing jeans and sweatshirt, tennis shoes, a pea jacket, Sylvia carried one airline bag. The famous green eyes were the giveaway.

"Sylvia?"

Two abrupt nods and then, chin on her chest, looking at

17

the floor, she said, "Sister Mary Teresa is expecting me."

If the actress had been trouble before in all the glory of stardom, she was in this incarnation an infinitely more demanding guest. She wanted to dress like Sister Mary Teresa.

"I don't think any of my habits would fit you, child."

Sylvia turned to Kim. She clearly disapproved of Kim's Oxford gray suit and polka dot blouse. Joyce came in to see the celebrity and was surprised to find her sartorial twin.

"One of you can lend me a habit, can't you?"

"Not me," Joyce said. "We voted not to wear it and that was good enough for me."

"You don't even own one?"

Kim and Joyce confessed that they did not.

"But Sister Mary Teresa . . ."

"One could retain the traditional habit if one desired, Sylvia. I of course did not choose to change."

"I must wear a habit. It's no good if I just dress like anyone else. Nuns should look like nuns."

Emtee Dempsey beamed at such sound doctrine. "Indeed. But the important thing is to be what one seems."

"I'll have one made."

"Better order a Carmelite habit, Sylvia. It's what you'll be wearing in the film."

Sylvia agreed and looked to the window. Was she thinking she should have chosen a Carmelite convent in which to accustom herself to her role?

"Show me where I'll be staying, let me take a copy of your rule and I'll go get a habit. Theatrical costume suppliers should have what I want."

It was Kim's idea that Sylvia take the apartment in the basement which would give her privacy and where there was a television.

Sylvia shuddered. "No television. My Carmelites did not have television."

So Kim showed Sylvia to a room on the second floor whose lack of austerity disappointed her.

"Let me see Sister Mary Teresa's room." Sylvia was whispering.

In Emtee Dempsey's room was a single bed, a chair, a prie-dieu.

"This is what I want!" Sylvia cried. Kim promised to reduce the guest room to the same uncluttered condition and Sylvia called a cab and was off to find a habit.

Emtee Dempsey was at work in her study, so Kim went into the kitchen to have a cup of coffee.

"Did you ever dress up as a nun when you were a kid?" Joyce asked.

"When I was a kid becoming a nun was the farthest thing from my mind." Encountering Emtee Dempsey had planted the seed of her vocation.

"Just asking. Neither did I. All the girls I knew who dressed up as nuns got over it by the time they were teenagers."

"Are you suggesting a parallel?"

"If the habit fits . . ."

Sylvia had come to the house at two-thirty; she had left again shortly after three. The idea was that she would be back in no time. But an hour went by, two hours, and then it was six, and no Sylvia Corrigan.

"Where has she been staying, I wonder?" Emtee Dempsey said.

Joyce said, "I could call *Kup's Show*."

But the talk show had no idea what hotel Sylvia had gone to on arriving in Chicago. So all they could do was wait.

They delayed supper until seven and then went ahead, but it was a joyless meal with three sets of ears cocked to hear the doorbell or at least the phone. They had not heard from Sylvia when the time for night prayers came and the three went to the chapel for Compline.

That night Kim did not sleep, thinking that this strange development must be keeping Sister Mary Teresa awake, but in the morning on the way to Mass at the cathedral the old nun said she had slept like a top. She did not mention Sylvia.

Sylvia was not mentioned at breakfast either and afterward in the study Emtee Dempsey looked at a note on her desk.

"I was going to ask you to bring me Molnar's book on Bernanos, but I suppose we can let that wait."

"What do you suppose happened?"

"I have no idea." And then her eyes looked at Kim through round gold-rimmed glasses. "But I don't like it. I don't like it at all."

Before Kim set out for the university, the phone rang. It was her brother Richard, a detective on the Chicago police department, full of early morning cheer. "You're not missing a nun, are you, Kim?"

"Don't be funny."

"Just checking. There's one in the morgue, all dressed up in the old habit, and we can't find where she belongs."

"In the morgue?"

"That's where we put dead nuns when we find them lying around in public places."

"Richard, listen. Sister Mary Teresa and I are going to the morgue. Meet us there."

"Do you know who it is?"

Kim hesitated. "I can't say. Will you be there?"

"Look, Kim, I don't have time . . ."

"Richard Moriarity!"

"You sound like Mom. Okay. I'll be there."

"Where is the morgue, Richard?"

Emtee Dempsey listened in silence as Kim told her of Richard's call. She rose in silence from her chair, took her cane, and thumped down the hall toward the front door. Wedged into the passenger seat of the battered VW bug, she rode in silence as Kim headed for the address Richard had given her.

Kim knew the old nun approved what she had done and the swiftness with which she had decided. But neither of them wanted to speculate. It was too dreadful, too bizarre a possibility. Yet it would have been impossible not to make the connection after what Richard had said. How many nuns in traditional costume are there anymore?

Richard was standing impatiently on the steps, squinting in the autumn sunlight, anxious to get this over with. He hustled them right into the viewing room, asked Emtee Dempsey if she could see the monitor all right, then called through to the attendant.

The body was shown as it had been found, clothed in a religious habit. The face looked fuller because of the headdress. The profile was unmistakable. But Emtee Dempsey asked, "What color are the eyes?"

"Green," came the answer.

Kim had turned away when the televised hand moved to the dead woman's eyes.

"There's no doubt, Richard. That is the body of Sylvia Corrigan."

He looked at her, he looked at Kim, he began to smile and then grew stern.

"Sylvia Corrigan the actress?"

21

"That's right. She's an alumna of the college. She visited us yesterday in mid-afternoon. She'd intended to spend some time with us on Walton Street."

"But she's dressed as a nun."

"She's an actress," Emtee Dempsey said.

He decided that was enigmatic enough to serve as an explanation. He took another look at the two of them, as if hoping to surprise some clue that they were kidding him, then went into action. On the phone.

Sister Mary Teresa stood for a moment, looking at the face that still appeared on the screen, and her mouth moved in prayer. When she was through, she said, "Let's go back to the house."

The return drive was silent but for one remark of the old nun. "She was going to play a nun who was killed. As usual, she entered into the role completely."

2

Sylvia Corrigan's death was a journalistic sensation and not even Emtee Dempsey had it in her to blame the media for their treatment of it. What else could one expect in a post-Christian age? As nuns became less numerous, they acquired box office appeal. Movies, plays, novels of a sort, have appeared in incredible numbers playing the changes on the Maria Monk legends of yore. The old nun's considered judgment was that as a group they had been treated with excessive respect in the past and this was God's way of righting the balance. Our Lord too, she reminded Kim and Joyce, had come to a bad end, in a worldly sense. That an actress of Sylvia Corrigan's renown should be found dead in a nun's habit on a Chicago street corner stimulated the jaded pens of journalists from coast to coast. A persistent theory was that she had really been a nun all along.

"You will not read such nonsense in the *Tribune*," Katherine Senski fumed, her sherry dipping from rim to rim in her glass, though she did not spill a drop. "Can you imagine! They actually believe a nun could be an actress."

But her old friend Emtee Dempsey did not share Katherine's indignation. It was not often these old warriors were at odds, but this was one of them. Katherine, in the same decade of her life as Emtee Dempsey, was the doyenne of Chicago journalism, and still active. She had been a trustee of the college and fought its closing at Emtee Dempsey's side. Defeat had brought them even closer together and Katherine was a frequent visitor on Walton Street.

"I shall never understand you," she said impatiently, after Emtee Dempsey's accounts of the Little Flower starring as Joan of Arc in the Carmel of Lisieux and of the singer who joined a convent in the Bois de Boulogne with the result that half of Paris filled the chapel during Holy Week when the former diva sang.

"Let us forget generalities about the degree of disrespect now shown the religious life, and speak of the case before us." Sylvia had been strangled. This had not been immediately apparent because the ugly results had been covered by her wimple.

"A fastidious murderer," Katherine said.

"How do you mean?"

"Concealing what he did."

"Indeed." Emtee Dempsey looked at Kim. She might have been asking her not to reveal how she'd had to work every item out of Richard by wiles, by food and drink, and the promise that she would not, for once in her life, interfere in police business. "From what Richard tells us, she could not have been wearing the habit when she was strangled."

"Good heavens!"

"I am not sure Richard and the police realize that."

"Are you suggesting she was dressed up in the habit after she was killed?"

"I am. And then left sitting on a bench at an intersection in the loop."

Katherine finished her sherry and held out the empty glass to Kim. "Sister, please. Every death is terrible, but to think that we are talking of Sylvia Corrigan."

One of the premiere alumnae of the college, that is, and a person of whom they had been so proud for so long. Before Kim left the room, Katherine asked Emtee Dempsey if she had met Raoul St.-Loup, the agent and publicist.

"My dear, that is why you were invited. I am expecting him tonight."

Raoul St.-Loup did not pretend that he took worthless clay and molded it into a celebrity. All of his clients had already attained some claim on public attention before he represented them. He would not have taken them on otherwise. But it was his boast that every client of his received the benefit of his own considerable abilities and that each had achieved as much celebrity as he or she was capable of or, in some cases, wanted. Sylvia Corrigan had been a promising actress when he took her on; within a few years she was a star in the theatrical firmament. Let his enemies make of that what they would.

"I am devastated by what has happened," he sighed, when they were settled in the living room, Emtee Dempsey in her high back brocade chair, Katherine and Raoul on one of the couches flanking the fireplace, Kim across from them. St.-Loup brought the long fingers of one hand to his forehead as he spoke, revealing a thick gold chain on his right wrist. There was another at his neck, visible because of his open collar—actually his shirt was unbuttoned to such an extent that the luxuriant hair on his chest was all too visible. What he wore could not be called a suit. The cut of the coat was odd, extremely full, the material had the look of corduroy but was black velvet. His trousers hugged his legs and his elegant feet were enclosed in a kind of boot. He moved his hand from his forehead through his tousled hair.

"I realize that no one here will admit to a belief in astrology, but I warned Sylvia not to come to Chicago. For a Libra at this time—well, you see what has happened."

"Nonsense," Emtee Dempsey said. "She was not strangled by a star."

Raoul smiled sweetly at her, as if approving such loyalty to her benighted beliefs.

Katherine said, "I had the impression she was fleeing trouble on the coast."

They had all learned a lot about Sylvia in the past twenty-four hours, and the colorful life she led was something of a surprise. They had known she never married, but Kim was startled to learn that the actress had never been without a lover. Half a dozen shared the spotlight her death had created. Two of them were dead, one in a plane crash, another from an overdose of drugs. Of the four remaining, three gave unctuous accounts to the press of what a splendid person Sylvia had been. References to what it was like to live with her, while indiscreet, seemed meant in praise.

"Nick Faustino must be eating his heart out," Raoul said, leaning toward Katherine and putting a hand on her arm. Perhaps it was the tenor of the conversation, but Katherine, in her seventies, reacted as if the publicist, not yet forty, were making an indecent approach. He patted her arm and withdrew his hand. "I warned him not to bring that suit."

"That suit" had been another indication that Sylvia's life did not incorporate the ideal that had been put before her at the M&M's college. Faustino had brought a palimony suit against her, seeking a settlement for the nearly two years they had lived together.

"It may have stretched over two years," Raoul said, in a pickwickian defense of Sylvia's honor, "but it was just a weekend now and then. I don't think he ever moved in."

Such allegations against an honored alumna were bad; also bad was Faustino's inclusion of Jimmy Horan in his suit, as the one who had alienated Sylvia's affections. Joyce had been able to provide them with a circumstanced portrait of Horan.

Jimmy Horan was the son of a member of the Irish mafia in Hollywood and had been brought up to consider Cagney and Tracy and O'Brien as uncles. His father too had been married to but one woman with whom he had had five children. Any general statement about the laxness of morals among film actors was sure to be met with the counter example of Jimmy Horan Sr. For nearly twenty years, at Easter, he and his family had appeared in a television special, a show that Emtee Dempsey had called, the one time she watched it, "the apotheosis of wholesomeness." For Faustino to suggest that Jimmy Horan was involved in some illicit way with Sylvia Corrigan was a little like maligning the family and spitting on the flag.

"Of course it backfired on Faustino," Raoul St.-Loup said. "I knew it would hurt him. That is why I didn't warn him."

"Is Faustino a client of yours?" Emtee Dempsey asked.

"Not any more."

Despite these preliminaries, the evening with Raoul St.-Loup proved more than informative. Joyce's beef roast with artichoke and the Italian red wine, a Barolla, a gift of their lawyer Mr. Rush, had much to do with this. Early the next morning Katherine sent the summary she had made of the conversation to Walton Street by special messenger. Emtee Dempsey read it with approval.

1. Faustino was wrong to accuse Jimmy Horan of alienating Sylvia's affections, but there was another man in the picture, one whose identity was unknown even to Raoul St.-Loup. ("Think of me as a confessor," he quoted himself as saying to his clients. "Tell me all your sins. It doesn't matter. With me you can do no wrong. But I must know everything so that nothing can hurt you." A dubious theology, whatever could be said of it as public relations.) Sylvia had broken this commandment—as well as ignoring the danger to a Libra in Chicago in this precise October—and look what had happened. In short, there was a new man in Sylvia's life.

2. The company with which Sylvia had played Medea was still in town. Her agreement had been to star on two occasions, at the Blackstone; she had been replaced by another actress, the play went on, though to considerably diminished audiences. Faustino was a member of the company.

3. Yet another of her one-time lovers was currently in Chicago. Brian Casey, the singer, was fulfilling a week's engagement in a loop bistro.

4. Raoul St.-Loup had also been in Chicago at the time, here to see Sylvia's second and last performance as Medea, but as well out of concern for her because of her astrological sign.

Added to this information, which Richard either already knew or would know, was the fact that Sylvia had rented a suite at the Elysian Hotel for a month, and had not instructed Maude Howe, her secretary, maid, confidante, girl Friday, to pack her things and return to the coast. If Sylvia hoped to live on Walton Street, she would continue to be registered at the Elysian. There seemed little doubt that the strangling had taken place in her hotel suite.

"Was there a struggle?"

Richard shook his head. "The room wasn't torn up. But she did not die easily by the look of the bed."

Emtee Dempsey had an appetite for details on such matters that Kim did not share so she adjourned to the kitchen to be with Joyce. Fat chance.

"Bring Richard a beer," Emtee Dempsey said when Kim left the room.

"He's already had a beer," Kim said, but she was looking at her brother. Richard knew that it was unwise for Moriaritys to drink. He should also know that the old nun was plying him with Heinekens to get more information out of him.

When Kim returned, Emtee Dempsey was summing up.

"Her publicist was here in Chicago, her secretary was here, others who knew her were here. Yet no one reported her missing? No one was surprised that she did not return?"

"No one reported her missing," Richard said. "It wasn't that long a time."

"All night?" But the old nun dropped her eyes. "Perhaps in her circle that would not have been considered long."

When Richard left, she looked at Kim. "You know what you must do now."

Kim looked at Emtee Dempsey, who was already preparing to begin her day's stint on her medieval history, a fresh sheet of paper before her, a giant fountain pen in her chubby hand.

"What do I know I must do?"

Blue eyes appeared over the gold-rimmed spectacles. "Go have a talk with Maud Howe, of course."

3

Maud Howe was in her mid twenties, a strawberry blonde with a face that seemed freshly scrubbed, pale blue eyes that looked right at Kim, and dimples when she smiled. Which she did when Kim told Maud that she was a nun.

"Funny."

"I'm quite serious. Sylvia Corrigan attended our college. She visited us the day this terrible thing happened. She asked if she could stay—"

Maud held up her hand. "I know all that. You're really a nun?" She shook her head. "So why did Sylvia have to rent that elaborate get up? You dress like anyone else."

Meaning Maud wasn't much of a dresser herself. She was wearing light blue corduroy slacks, loafers, a heavy knit blouse. How an outdoor girl like her had ended up with the job she had was not obvious.

"Sylvia played a tennis pro in *Love Match* and I coached her. She kept me on. It has been a very lively couple of years."

"How many?"

"Four."

"I'm supposed to ask you why you didn't report Sylvia missing."

"Supposed to ask?"

Kim explained about Emtee Dempsey. Maud nodded. "She's the one Sylvia told me about. I assumed there was a house full of you dressed like her."

"The story in which Sylvia was supposed to play a nun is set at the time of the French Revolution. She would have had to wear a traditional habit."

"Well, she got one."

"Where?"

"Hanson's. They specialize in supplying wardrobes for theatrical productions. Sylvia figured they'd have a religious habit, and she was right."

"Tell me about it."

"You mean, the time, all that? You too?"

"I suppose you've had to tell the police this already."

"And everybody else."

"Like who?"

"All her friends who are in Chicago have wanted to know." And she ticked off names they had already heard from Raoul St.-Loup. Of course Maud's list included St.-Loup as well. "To answer your first question, the reason I didn't report her missing was because I knew she meant to spend the night with you."

"So what did you do?"

"You'd think I'd take a bath and go to bed with a good book, wouldn't you? I don't have that many chances just to relax. But I went down to hear Brian sing."

"Maud, who do you think did it?"

"I know who did it!"

"Who?"

"Nick Faustino. Don't ask me how he got in here. I can't imagine that Sylvia would let him in, but he has the guts of a burglar anyway. He hung around her until she finally got rid of him, almost physically, and then he brought that absurd law suit."

"It isn't true?"

"That they were lovers? I won't deny that. But he claims he lived with her. That he devoted himself to her career at the expense of his own. His career! And then that stupid story about Jimmy Horan. It's almost as if he doesn't want to be believed."

"If he hoped to get money from her, why would he kill her?"

"I don't know. Why do people write on phone booth walls and do other dumb things? Perhaps he just convinced himself he had lived with Sylvia and someone replaced him."

"Isn't that true?"

For the first time her eyes slid away. "You can't replace someone who never held a place."

"Did you tell the police about Faustino?"

"Did I ever."

"Is there any evidence at all that he did it?"

"Well, they certainly looked the place over."

"Maud, she wasn't wearing the habit when she was killed."

Maud studied Kim for half a minute. "They know that?"

Kim nodded. "Who is the new man?"

The eyes began to slide again, but she stopped them. "I don't know. I really don't. It's the first big secret she kept from me since I started working for her."

"But you have a guess?"

She laughed. "Several."

"Then why aren't there several possibilities of people who might have killed her?"

"I guess there are. I could have done it."

"What motive?"

"For stealing Jimmy Horan away from me." Her grin was contagious.

"You have to come visit us on Walton Street."

"Would I have to wear a habit?"

"I don't recommend it."

But thoughts of Sylvia drove away the smiles. On the way back to Walton Street, Kim wondered if Maud Howe was really sad her employer was dead. So far there seemed no genuine mourners for Sylvia Corrigan. People said things, things that sounded half-rehearsed. But no one acted as if the death of Sylvia was cause for weeping.

The face of the man sitting in the chair opposite Sister Mary Teresa's desk was both familiar and legendary, the face of someone Kim felt she had long known. It was Brian Casey the singer, one of the men in Sylvia Corrigan's life. He rose when Emtee Dempsey told him who Kim was, but his face was a tragic mask, mouth downturned, eyes sad.

"Mr. Casey informs me that the mystery is solved, Sister Kimberly."

"Maud Howe thinks Nick Faustino did it."

Casey plunged his face into his hands. "Oh, if only he had."

"Mr. Casey has just confessed to me that he murdered Sylvia Corrigan."

The famous face lifted from his hands and he looked woefully at Kim. Emtee Dempsey continued, "The question is, Sister, should he confess to the police?"

"But you were singing last night. Maud Howe went to see you."

"Yes, I know. And she did. But I slipped away between sets. The club is only a block from the Elysian."

"He walked," Emtee Dempsey said, and it was clear to Kim that she did not believe the singer.

"I came to Sister Mary Teresa because Sylvia and I were speaking of her just before the argument broke out. I had to tell someone."

"Were you surprised to find her in a religious habit?" Kim asked.

"Part of the sordidness of this is that I found her more attractive as a nun. I don't mean to shock you. And then we argued, I became furious and . . ." He stopped for air. "It makes it so much worse, killing someone I love, killing someone in a religious habit."

"Strangling her."

He nodded, then again covered his face with his hands. Emtee Dempsey and Kim exchanged a look. "I think you should wait before going to the police," the old nun said.

"What's the difference, sooner or later?"

"Have you ever been in jail?"

He looked up. "No."

"Later is better. Anyone will tell you that."

Kim assumed the old nun was trying to come up with a way of finding out why Brian Casey was telling this so easily disprovable story. It was clear that he knew only what had appeared in the newspapers. As the time for his evening performance neared he grew more willing to postpone calling the police. Emtee Dempsey assured him he should go to the club and entertain, but the way she said it made it clear she could not fathom why adults would sit around in an ill-lit, smoke-filled room listening to even so good a singer as Brian Casey croon outdated songs. Kim went with him to the door. On the porch he turned his sad face to her once more. "I feel like Pagliacci," he said.

"Laughing on the outside?"

"Crying on the inside! I sing that." And went off into the night, crooning the golden oldie.

The next morning, on the way back from Mass, Emtee Dempsey told Kim to stop for a newspaper. Back in the car, she was reluctant to give it to the old nun until she herself had read the story. Emtee Dempsey said, "If you read it aloud we could all know what has happened."

From the back seat, Joyce said, "You can't stand people

who read the newspaper at you."

"I can when they won't give it to me."

Kim gave the paper over. Let Emtee Dempsey read it aloud. Numbed, she started the car and continued to the house.

4

The death of Brian Casey after he had visited her following Sylvia Corrigan's murder, which had also occurred after a visit to Walton Street lit a fire in Emtee Dempsey. This had become doubly a personal matter now and she was over whatever inaction the news of Sylvia's private life had induced. No matter how she had lived, she had been ignobly murdered. And now Brian Casey, a perfectly harmless man, was also dead.

"But why did he come here saying he had killed her?"

"Why does anyone falsely confess to a murder?"

"Is there only one reason?"

"It is overwhelmingly likely to be because the one confessing is shielding another he thinks guilty. It may very well be that the element of truth in the man's story is that he did go to the Elysian Hotel between his entertainment sessions and that while there he saw the murder or saw something that made him conclude who the murderer is. In either case, it is someone he wishes to shield from harm."

Kim tried unsuccessfully to stop the image of Maud Howe's face from forming in her mind. But if Maud came easily to mind as someone Brian might wish to protect, it was impossible to believe she needed it. And, on the hypothesis Emtee Dempsey was exploring, Maud would have to be the murderer not only of one person but of two. Whoever Brian Casey had been trying to protect had in the end killed him because his knowledge posed a threat.

"He confessed because he thought the other person would easily be suspected?"

"But he didn't quite confess, did he? He told me things, and he repeated them to you. But the only risk he really ran was that you or I would feel compelled to tell the police what he had said. And what would he have done then?"

"Do you think he was that devious?"

The old nun smiled. "Sister Kimberly, we are all born devious. Our task is to overcome it by acquiring honesty and other virtues. I myself might be tempted to deviousness in certain circumstances and who is to say I should not fall?"

"His telling us was insurance?"

"Don't dismiss the possibility. We'll never get to the bottom of this if you pretend to be surprised at the human capacity for iniquity." Emtee Dempsey might have been chiding herself for her reaction to the revelations of Sylvia's irregular life.

The life Sylvia had led raised questions about her funeral, but in the end it was decided to err on the side of mercy and Sylvia was buried from the cathedral. An auxiliary bishop of Chicago was in the sanctuary but the Mass was said by a Los Angeles priest with golden hair, a tanned complexion and a dental ad smile who flew in from the coast for the occasion. Father Estrella, identified in the papers as Sylvia's pastor.

"Spiritual director would be more accurate," Father Estrella told Kim when she engaged him in conversation. Emtee Dempsey wanted to speak to the "media priest."

"A friend of Sylvia's? Of course. Let's see." And out came an appointment book he opened and frowned over. "My being in Chicago is not much of a secret," he said in explanation.

"Sylvia had intended to stay with us as she readied herself for the Bernanos' role."

His mouth opened and he pointed a finger at her. "Why didn't you say so? I want to meet Sister Mary Teresa."

She drove him there in the VW. At first he thought it was a joke but he got in. The motor took a while to start and he suggested a cab, but then it caught and she wheeled away from the curb and they were on their way.

"I didn't think any of these were still around."

"This one belonged to Herman Goering, according to Joyce."

"Joyce is one of the sisters?"

"That's right."

"Herman couldn't have gotten half a ham into this seat, I guarantee you. Tell me a bit about the old nun."

"What have you heard?"

"She was one of Sylvia's favorite people, that's for sure. Her conscience. Whenever she thought of taking her religion seriously again. She was practicing again of late, thank God."

"Did you hear how she died?"

"The strangling?"

"She wasn't dressed in the habit when she was killed."

"I see. Well, well. You're suggesting that the killer, having strangled her, dressed her up in a religious habit?"

"And put her on a bench in the Loop."

"Why on earth would he do that?"

"That is one of the questions Emtee Dempsey wants to put to you."

"The only bell that rings is that Sylvia's first appearance on film was a bit part in *Bus Stop*."

Emtee Dempsey found that uninteresting. Kim was a little annoyed that the old nun seemed more interested in quizzing

Estrella about his ministry in California than about Sylvia Corrigan.

If the priest hadn't brought up the murder she wondered if Emtee Dempsey would have. But once Sylvia was mentioned, the questions began.

"Father, who killed her?"

He smiled, creating deep dimples in his tanned cheeks. "You want me to make a guess?"

"Is it safe to rule out Jimmy Horan?"

"Good Lord, yes."

"And now Brian is gone. That leaves a narrowed field."

"You can eliminate Samuelson, Hoague and Jensen too, Sister."

"On what basis?"

"Well, it is not generally known but Samuelson is a homosexual. Sylvia permitted the rumors of an affair to circulate in order to help him keep his secret. It's not entirely a secret anymore, of course."

"And Hoague?"

"How often do former lovers remain friends?"

"I have no idea."

He smiled. "I suppose not. I can tell you it is infrequent. But Sylvia and Larry Hoague were genuinely an exception. He would not have harmed her for the world. He was one of the few people who encouraged her to do Medea here and it was a triumph, or so I am told."

As for Jensen, he was not in Chicago and could not have been the night of the strangling because he was taking religious instructions from Father Estrella.

"It was an effect of knowing Sylvia. Feelings of guilt would bring her religious faith to the surface and she and Jensen talked about it. He became interested. He came to me. It's the reason the affair ended. Sylvia thought that should earn her credit in the great box office in the sky."

"She may be right," Emtee Dempsey said thoughtfully. "Now that leaves Faustino and St.-Loup."

"Sylvia was St.-Loup's meal ticket. From the time he landed her a part in *Bus Stop* he concentrated on her as his main client. And he was right. If he represented no one else, he would be a rich man. Sylvia recognized his value to her and rewarded him. I think he was written in for ten percent, just like an agent. But then, increasingly, that is how he functioned for her."

"She had no other agent?"

"No."

"Father, you were reluctant to make a guess as to who did it, but what you say suggests that Faustino killed Sylvia and Brian."

If the conclusion surprised him, he did not show it. Then he said softly, "If I had guessed, I would have said Faustino."

5

The police had come to the same conclusion. Faustino was arrested on the steps of the cathedral after attending the funeral.

"I wonder what evidence they have," Kim said.

Emtee Dempsey squeezed her eyes shut. "So do I."

"Should I call Richard?"

Her eyes opened. "You are volunteering? I was trying to think of a way to persuade you to invite him here that would not give you an opportunity to repeat your usual objections."

"I want to know."

"Of course. 'All men by nature desire to know.' Aristotle. Call him."

"Aristotle?"

The old nun pushed the phone toward Kim, giving her a look. "Being with theatrical folk has a bad effect on you, Sister Kimberly."

Richard was not offended by her suggestion that he stop by Walton Street. He was clearly happy to have swiftly settled on a prime suspect in the double murder.

Richard having agreed to come, Emtee Dempsey decided it would be nice to have Katherine Senski there as well. "Oh, and ask Maud Howe to come."

"Richard might not like that."

"Why not? A slightly larger audience for him when he relates his triumph."

Was she being sarcastic? Richard arrived and she congratulated him warmly and when Katherine came, and later Maud, she presented Richard as if he were the quintessence of effective police investigation.

"We're all just dying to hear how you learned it was Faustino."

"No more dying, now. Not in my jurisdiction." He smiled at Maud. Maud, it was evident, was the one Richard most wished to impress. Shame on him. Kim would get in a mention of his wife and children if he kept it up.

"How did you know it was Faustino?" Maud could play the ingenue role pretty effectively.

"I'd like to tell you it took a lot of thinking, a lot of lab work, a lot of patient routine. I am a great champion of routine. Most police work is fairly humdrum stuff, no mystery at all, except in trying to figure out what the judge and jury might do."

Emtee Dempsey cleared her throat. She knew a lecture when she heard one. Not that she was often on the listening end.

"The truth is he couldn't have made it more obvious that he had done it."

"How so?" Maud asked.

"Three things. First, we found another religious habit in his hotel room. It had come from Hanson's and sure enough, she had rented two. Bought them, rather. She didn't want to rent. He must have taken that away with him. Don't ask me why." He looked around as if paragraphs of a manual of sexual pathology were rolling past his mind. "Second, his fingerprints were found in the suite."

Maud said, "He came by the day before it happened. They might have been made then."

Richard smiled, unperturbed. "That's why it is so convenient that the doorman saw him leave the Elysian near or slightly after the time the coroner places the murder."

"Carrying a box?"

Richard had expected applause, not questions, but he managed a tight smile. "I wouldn't want you too easily convinced, Sister Mary Teresa. But when you add these things up, you've got a prima facie case. I think Faustino is ready to tell us all about it."

"Brian Casey was ready to do that."

"What do you mean?"

"He told me and Sister Kimberly most solemnly that he had killed Sylvia."

"Why would he say a thing like that?"

But it was Maud who answered. "The dope probably thought I did it and wanted to make the ultimate sacrifice." Her voice broke. "And now he really has."

Emtee Dempsey was usually intolerant of tears, but on this occasion she got up and went to Maud and put her arm around her shoulder.

"So it was you he was protecting?"

She bobbed her head and got herself under control. "I haven't told you everything," she said to Richard, and glanced at Kim as well. "I found Sylvia that night. I came in and called for her and she didn't answer and then when I went into her room . . ." She broke down again.

"There, there. Just take your time and tell us," the old nun said soothingly.

"She was dead! The bed was all torn apart and I tried her pulse and there was no point in calling an ambulance. Then I panicked."

"And went to the club where Brian was entertaining."

"Yes."

Richard said, "Why did you panic?"

"I couldn't stay there with her. She was dead."

Maud looked at Richard as if trying to convey to him what it had been like to be in the same room with the corpse of the woman for whom she had worked. "I was frightened, because she was dead. Just a few hours before we'd been talking and now she wasn't there anymore, only her body." She shuddered.

"You were afraid only because she was dead?" Richard asked.

She snuffled and nodded her head.

"Then why did Brian think he had to protect you?"

"Because I'd had an argument with Sylvia that morning. We were always having arguments. But he was there and overheard it and worried it would seem worse than it was."

"To him?"

"Faustino was there too."

Richard said, "Tell me. Did Brian Casey go to the Elysian between sets or not?"

"When I told him what had happened he went to see if she was really dead."

"Did he move the body?"

"No! He was almost as shaken as I was."

"Did he dress the body?"

Maud looked up at Richard. "That was the strange part. He said he found her lying on the bed dressed in a nun's habit. I told him that was impossible. She was wearing only panties and a bra when I found her. But he insisted."

Sister Mary Teresa said to Richard, "Well, you have a thing or two to ask Mr. Faustino, don't you?"

Richard made a thin line with his lips. Being instructed by Emtee Dempsey on how to do his job was almost more than he could bear. "I want you to come along with me, Miss Howe. Let's get all this down on paper."

"She should have a lawyer," Katherine said and met Richard's glare defiantly. "I am not suggesting you use torture, Lieutenant Moriarity. It is simply better all around that she have counsel before making statements."

"I will call Mr. Rush," Emtee said.

She did and their lawyer arranged to meet Richard and Maud downtown.

"I'll come along," Kim said. Maud still looked shaken.

"That isn't necessary," the young woman said.

"Nonsense," Emtee Dempsey said, always willing to volunteer Kim's services. "Of course Sister will accompany you."

6

Katherine was still at the house when Kim returned and the reporter looked a little under the influence of the sherry she had been drinking.

"Oh good, Kim, you're back. I've been refusing to leave until I have a witness to what this impossible old woman has told me."

"Katherine," said Emtee Dempsey, sipping her tea. "I

have no idea why you make such a fuss about it."

"Oh don't you? Kim, Sister Mary Teresa has told me that she knows who killed Sylvia Corrigan and Brian Casey."

"You heard Richard, Katherine. They've arrested Nick Faustino." How much sherry had Katherine had?

"But she says it isn't Faustino!"

Emtee Dempsey smiled sweetly toward where the horizon would be if the wall hadn't been in the way. "Of course it isn't."

"Then who is it?" Kim asked.

The old nun took her watch from the pocket concealed by her wimple and pressed its stem to open it. "It is nearly eleven o'clock. Much too late for revelations. Besides, I could not corroborate it now. But I will be able to tell you before noon tomorrow."

"Oh, posh," Katherine said. "You're showboating."

"I wonder what the origin of that expression is?" Emtee Dempsey said, apparently genuinely curious.

"You're changing the subject."

"I will do what I said I would do before noon tomorrow. Would you like to join us for night prayers, Katherine?"

"No," the reporter said, rising and then steadying herself. "This old sinner is going home to bed."

"Sister Kimberly will get you a cab."

It was difficult in chapel, during Compline, to fight distraction. Emtee Dempsey recited the psalms with obvious relish. She loved the office. Did she really know who had killed those two people? How could she? Kim knew as much, maybe more, than the old nun did. And, like Maud Howe, who certainly knew more than both of them, she was satisfied that the police had the killer in custody. If not Faustino, who?

She shook her head, trying not to feel annoyance at Emtee Dempsey. The old nun was showboating, as Katherine had said.

But later, in bed, staring wide awake at the ceiling, Kim went over everything she knew about the two murders.

Sylvia Corrigan had left the house on Walton Street, gone to Hanson's and purchased two religious habits, gone to her hotel, taken off her secular clothes to try on a habit and been strangled before she got it on. (No need to speculate about anything leading up to her being found dead in bed.) Maud discovered her in bra and panties and fled to tell Brian. He hurried to the Elysian and found the dead body of Sylvia, now clothed in a religious habit. He returned to the club and hours later the body was found seated on a bench on a Loop corner, for all the world as if Sylvia were waiting for a bus. The following day, Brian Casey came to Emtee Dempsey saying he had killed Sylvia, but his story suggested that he did not realize she had been strangled before the habit had been put on her.

Presumably he was just hedging so as not to draw attention to the difference between the body as Maud found it and as he found it less than half an hour later. Is that what Emtee Dempsey had concluded? But on what basis? Such guessing could only begin once one excluded Faustino, but why exclude him?

Even after she fell asleep Kim dreamed of Emtee Dempsey's claim and she spent a restless night dreaming up ways of disproving it. And before she said anything to anyone else. Kim lived in dread that one day Sister Mary Teresa would make such a statement and be proved wrong, with devastating effects to her prestige and—though this was less likely—her self-esteem.

7

The following morning, despite Emtee Dempsey's flamboyant promise to produce a murderer other than Nick Faustino before lunch, nothing much happened. After breakfast, the old nun went to work on her history of the 12th century, prepared to add her daily quota of handwritten pages. Did she have anything she wished Kim to do? The great headdress moved in negation.

"Maud is in danger, Sister," Kim blurted out. "If the murderer killed Casey, he'll kill her for the same reason."

The old nun looked up. "Katherine Senski had the same thought. Maud is at Katherine's apartment, not the Elysian Hotel."

"Then you think Maud's innocent?"

"She is a daughter of Eve," Emtee Dempsey said enigmatically. "As are we all."

A little miffed, Kim went upstairs to her room where, at her own desk, she tried to ignore the light on the phone that told her someone in the house was making calls. It was difficult to concentrate.

The case against Maud looked worse in daylight than it had in her troubled sleep. At ten-thirty, Kim went down for a cup of coffee, intending to talk to Joyce about it, but the front doorbell rang before she got out a cup and she hurried into the front hall.

Raoul St.-Loup stood on the porch, looking intently at the door as if he meant to open it with psychic power.

"I must see Sister Mary Teresa," he announced when Kim opened the door.

"You heard they arrested Nick Faustino?"

"I am more concerned about Maud Howe. She has disappeared."

Emtee Dempsey came out of her study and beckoned to her caller. Kim followed along but a small hand went up. "Sister, you might telephone Father Estrella to see if there have been any developments."

"Ask if he knows where Maud has gone," Raoul St.-Loup said, going into the study.

Feeling rebuffed, Kim went to the kitchen where after complaining to Joyce she put through the call to Father Estrella.

"Sister Mary Teresa wants to know if there have been any developments."

"I was about to put that question to her. She's the one with Chicago connections. Let me talk with her."

"Raoul St.-Loup is with her now, Father. He's worried about Maud Howe."

"Always the agent," the priest said, chuckling.

"How do you mean?"

"He thinks Maud's wholesome scrubbed countenance will be her fortune and the increase of his. He's been trying to wangle the part of Becky Thatcher in the scheduled remake of Tom Sawyer for her. Maybe he brought it off. Well, at least Sylvia was spared that."

"Don't tell me she wanted the role."

Father Estrella's laughter had a devilish lilt. "She was spared that remark too. No. But Sylvia had the usual ambiguous attitude toward the success of protégés."

"Meaning she was jealous."

"Sister, it is so refreshing to hear the capital sins mentioned without apology."

Father Estrella thought he might call Emtee Dempsey later. After Kim hung up, she accepted the cup of coffee

Joyce had thoughtfully poured for her.

"It's going on eleven, Kim."

"She's got an hour."

"Why does she brag like that?"

"Katherine is the only one she bragged to."

"And us."

"We don't count. We're family."

The buzzer sounded and Kim picked up the phone but there was no response from the study. She made a face at the receiver.

"Is she on?" Joyce asked.

Kim shook her head. The buzzer sounded again, insistently, but still the phone was dead.

"Joyce, something's wrong."

Joyce did not hesitate but took off for the study on the run with Kim following. Bursting into the study the way they did could have been the mistake of the half-century. But it wasn't.

St.-Loup was on Emtee Dempsey's side of the desk and his hands were seeking a firm position on her throat. Undignified as her position was, the old nun seemed calm. She had not cried out. But one finger pressed down the signal button of the phone.

With a well-placed chop on the inside of his right shoulder, Joyce dropped St.-Loup. He slid to the floor as if he were boneless. Kim helped the old nun back into her chair while Joyce dragged the agent into the middle of the study where she flipped him on his face, brought his wrists together behind him and tied them with the lace she removed from his suede boot.

"Call Katherine," Emtee Dempsey said in her normal voice when she was once more settled behind her desk. "She will be expecting to hear from me."

8

The following night Katherine, Maud Howe and Father Estrella came to the house on Walton Street for dinner. St.-Loup had been arrested and charged with the murders of Sylvia Corrigan and Brian Casey. Emtee Dempsey disdainfully rejected Richard's suggestion that she bring charges against the agent.

"There goes my career," Maud said.

"I would feel more sympathy if you had been candid with me, young lady," Sister Mary Teresa said.

"Will you play Becky Thatcher?" Father Estrella asked.

"Can St.-Loup represent me from prison?"

"There are those who would call prison the natural home of agents."

"There was a falling out between Sylvia and St.-Loup, wasn't there?" Emtee Dempsey said.

"Did Sylvia tell you that?"

"If she had, she might still be alive. No, it was St.-Loup. He seemed to think I would die happier knowing why he wished to kill me. He too was convinced Sylvia had revealed their falling out."

"Was it because of you?" Father Estrella asked Maud.

"Perhaps in part. He had made her a star, but what had he done for her lately, after all? He opposed her doing Medea and it was a smash. He mentioned *Bus Stop* once too often. She often ridiculed him to his face for that."

"Once too often perhaps," Katherine Senski said.

There was a moment of silence when they all seemed to be thinking of that oddly costumed corpse sitting on a bus stop bench in the loop.

"May she rest in peace," Emtee Dempsey said with emotion. "I for one shall always remember her as a college student doing *The Lady's Not For Burning*."

"I'm ready when you are," Joyce announced and they all went into the dining room.

Intent to Kill

He had often thought of killing Maud, in dreams and imagination, approaching the task with cold logic, carefully covering his tracks, getting it over with and then feigning inconsolable grief at the loss of his wife. Who would ever suspect him of being responsible for what would appear to be a quite natural, if tragic, occurrence?

Doing the deed in real life proved somewhat more taxing. For one thing, there was the terrified fear that turned his body clammy and made it difficult to recall the steps of the plan, even caused him to imagine that a dozen pairs of suspicious eyes were on him at all times.

Nonsense, of course, and he fought against the fear. After all, he had a double motive now. The longing to be rid of Maud had become so habitual that it seemed to concern himself alone, only his freedom, the shrugging off of the weight of her hateful presence and walking the earth a free man again.

He had long since given up the notion that others would understand his desire to be rid of his wife. She was beautiful; with others she was charming, even witty. Charles had watched men fall victim to her charms as she effortlessly enchanted them. It was all an act, of course. Once she had acted in the same way with him, but in those days neither of them realized that she was not serious, could not be serious, about such matters. Men were toys to play with and it would have been against her nature not to lure them.

Annoying but innocent. And, in its way, beneficial to him. Women sympathized with him as they fumed over Maud's triumphant domination of the room.

"She's so friendly," Catherine Willis had said, when he came upon her in the kitchen, dabbing at her eyes. In the living room, Maud was putting Fred Willis through her ringmaster's hoops.

"Only in public."

"Oh?"

"She's very good at parlor games."

"Just so they remain in the parlor."

"They always have."

"Are you sure?"

"Would we be talking like this if I weren't?"

It brought them together, Catherine Willis and himself, but of course that was only a little parlor game of their own. Sometimes he and Maud and the Willises made a foursome at golf and, when Maud pleaded with Fred to show her how to hold the club, how to swing it properly, just help her, please, Charles would drive away with Catherine in the golf cart they shared, sparing them both the spectacle. Just for fun they would mimic the antics Maud and Fred were engaged in. Standing behind Catherine while she putted, his arms around her, his hands gripping hers on the club, Charles felt a sudden dizziness and stepped back.

"Isn't this right?" Catherine asked saucily, looking back at him over her shoulder.

"Too right."

"Oh."

Small wonder that his fantasies about ridding himself of

Maud sometimes included a sequel in which he and Catherine, side by side in a golf cart, rode into the sunset together. He dismissed the thought. He did not intend to regain his freedom only to throw it away again before he had enjoyed it.

Enjoying it meant solitary global trips, alone in foreign cities, waiting for some unplanned adventure to happen. The point of freedom was that it be unpredictable.

Catherine called him at the office and asked him to take her to lunch. What could he do? He suggested they meet at the Club.

"I'm calling you from downtown. We don't want to drive all the way out there."

"Where would you like me to take you?"

"Horners."

Horners was a saloon overlooking the river. It had a very limited luncheon menu, was frequented by college kids, and sounded like lots of fun, a real break from routine. He said he'd meet her there.

"Oh no you won't. I took a cab downtown. Shall we meet in the lobby of your building?"

He suggested they meet in the garage where he parked his car.

"Were you afraid we'd be seen together?"

"Who suggested Horners?"

She laughed, then stopped abruptly. "Why am I laughing? It's not funny."

"What?"

"You lied to me."

"About what?"

"About Maud. About it being only a parlor game with her."

She gave him the gory details while they drank beer and

plucked greasy goodies from the plastic baskets they had ordered. A hamburger, dripping with number 30 oil, french fries ditto, bock beer. The lunch might have been a suicide pact.

"I have proof that they have gone to motels at least three times."

"Proof?"

"Credit card bills."

He looked at her. "Do your bills tell you who he was with?"

Catherine put the tip of a french fry between her sharp little teeth and nibbled it to death. After licking her fingers, she said, "I followed them."

He wanted to deny that this could be true, not to protect Maud's reputation, but to stave off the silly feeling Catherine's charges brought. Angry as he had been with Maud, hating her so much he wanted her dead, he had been complacent about her morals. Flirt, yes, she couldn't help it. But actually go off to a motel with another man? He felt the sharp sting reserved for the cuckold, a pain that does not require that the husband really give a damn about his wife. Maud had made a fool of him. It was like an extra reason to kill her.

And so finally he laid his plans, moving the project from dream and fantasy into the real world, feeling as a result terror and fear of apprehension, but feeling excitement too. It was a game played for great stakes. Success would mean either of two things—freedom, if he carried out his plan to perfection, or a far more definitive loss of freedom if he were suspected, charged, convicted, imprisoned. An emotion keener than fear came over him. He felt like a god, holding both Maud's fate and his own in his hands.

Her death must seem an accident, of course, but simply as a matter of insurance, a plausible suspect must be provided. Charles himself would be miles from the scene, of course, so far as anyone knew or could come to know. Given Maud's liaison with him, Fred would be on the scene and available as suspect if suspicion were indeed aroused. Fred seemed even more perfect as a target of suspicion in the light of Catherine's later information.

"It's over," she told him as they danced one evening at the club. "And no credit to Fred."

"Oh."

"Maud dumped him."

"He told you that?"

"I heard them on the phone."

"You eavesdropped?"

"Of course. Don't you?"

"Apparently there's no longer any reason to."

There was certainly no visible sign of a breach between Maud and Fred Willis. They had made a foursome for the club Mardi Gras dance, and Charles could look over Catherine's shoulder at his wife dancing with Fred, the couple apparently having the time of their lives.

But soon he had reason to think that Catherine was lying to him. He had Gorman, an investigator his law firm often employed, check out the motels Catherine claimed Maud and Fred had dallied in. It seemed it had never happened.

"Of course they wouldn't have used real names," Gorman reported with the certainty of a longtime student of infidelity. "But no one recognized their photographs either."

"Do you trust your informants?"

"No. I buy them."

Gorman was a longtime student of informers as well. Charles believed him and decided that Catherine was either flat out lying or imagining things. In any case, she now had conveniently removed what might have appeared to be his motivation for killing Maud. The imagined affair was over; they were all just friends again.

And it was time for Maud to die.

He arranged to be out of town. His secretary bought tickets well in advance of the Easter holiday. He arrived in Chicago to find O'Hare teeming with college kids and service personnel. The portion of his ticket to Chicago would be recorded as used; he had to insure the same for the Denver leg. A year ago at this time, he had been grateful that his ticket had been bought well in advance. Now he had a sure seat in first class. All around him in the oversold flight were kids destined to spend hours waiting for the next flight, maybe even spend the night in the terminal.

Charles checked in, took a seat and waited. This was a crucial part of his plan, yet it depended on something outside his control. Would this year be like the last? His doubts went as the waiting area filled up and kids began sprawling on the floor when there was nowhere else to wait. Eventually the announcement came. The flight was over-booked; anyone willing to surrender his seat would be given a credit toward a future flight within the continental United States. A groan greeted the announcement. Across from Charles, a young man looked wildly about. He wore a baseball cap backward on his head and had a bright blue and gold muffler wrapped around his neck.

"And I'm standby. I got to get home."

His remark was met with a minimum of sympathy, although solidarity among the passengers grew as the offer was renewed. The boy with the backward baseball cap went up to the counter to urge his case but after several minutes wandered away. Charles got up and caught up with the young man.

"I heard you say you had to get on this flight."

"There's no hope. They can't even promise me I'll get on the next one." There was genuine anguish in his voice.

"An emergency?"

He opened his mouth, then closed it. He grinned. "It is to me."

"How so?"

"My girl wants to break our engagement."

Charles would have preferred a more compelling emergency, but he didn't have time to seek a substitute.

"Look, I'll give you my seat assignment. I can stay over here. While waiting for the flight, I've been tempted by the thought of checking into the Hilton and getting a good night's rest."

"But what will you do tomorrow?"

"We'll just trade tickets."

"Can you just give me your assignment?" He looked anxiously back at the counter.

Charles smiled. He got out his ticket wallet. "Just use this. Go as me. You'll have to sit in first class though."

"First class!" The kid's eyes bugged.

"Shh. Take it." He handed the wallet to the kid, who almost immediately gave it back to him.

"I can't do that."

"I thought you had to get to Denver."

"I do."

"All right then."

His crisis of conscience was soon over. He took Charles's ticket and seat assignment, and handed over his own ticket. Charles suppressed a yawn, picked up his bag and told the kid he was headed for the O'Hare Hilton.

But when he came out of the concourse, he went down to

the street floor and bought a ticket on the shuttle back to Indiana. As he rode through the night, heading homeward to rid himself of Maud forever, he smiled at the thought that it would be a matter of record that he had taken the flight to Denver. Belatedly it occurred to him that checking into the Hilton would have certified his being away equally well. He could have gone to his room, messed up the bed, and left the hotel and hopped onto this shuttle bus. He would have been out some money, but less than for the plane ticket. Ah well. Next time. His smile was reflected in the window beside him.

The shuttle arrived at the airport of his hometown. Charles's car was in the parking lot. He drove to the 24-hour supermarket three blocks from his house, left his car in the parking lot and continued on foot. His house was dark when he approached it but there was still a light on next door at the Willises. He went around to the back of his house and let himself in quietly. Later he would create the appearance of a break-in. For now it was more important not to wake Maud.

He waited inside the back door and, when his eyes had adjusted to the darkness, moved swiftly through the house toward the stairway. Before he reached it, he tripped over something and went sprawling across the room, off balance. He crashed into a chair, overturning it, taking down a lamp as well. It fell onto the coffee table, scattering the gewgaws Maud kept on it. Charles struck his head against something and when he got to his feet and touched his forehead his hand came away sticky with blood. He went to the wall switch and turned it on. What he had stumbled over was the body of Maud.

Her eyes stared sightlessly at him from her discolored face. He stared at her for a full minute in the stark glare of the overhead light. Then he knelt beside her. She was definitely dead. A great wave of relief rolled through his mind bringing with it an indecent desire to shout for joy. He was innocently rid of Maud. She was dead and he hadn't killed her. He looked up the stairs, wondering if she had fallen, but then he saw the scarf twisted terribly around her throat. It looked to be one of his own.

He unwound it carefully and was standing with it in his hands when headlights swept in the drive and there was the sound of running toward the house. Someone pounded on the door. What the hell. He went to answer it. Hardly had he unlocked it, when a policeman pushed his way in and was followed by another. Charles was slammed against the wall and rapidly searched for weapons. Anger boiled up in him.

"What the hell are you doing? I live here."

"What's this?"

The second cop was looking down at Maud's body. He picked up the phone and made another call. In the still open doorway, Catherine appeared, wearing a robe, her eyes like saucers.

"Charles! What are you doing home?"

"Would you tell these maniacs that I live here?"

But Catherine was looking past him at Maud. Her mouth rounded in surprised horror. She looked at him.

"Oh, Charles. What have you done?"

His memory of what happened next was blurred, and try as he would to recall it accurately during the months he awaited trial it never quite came into focus. When he was indicted for the murder of Maud, he hired Gilligan, the best trial lawyer in town, a man whose knack for getting acquittals or risible sentences for clients that everyone knew were guilty as charged had hitherto excited Charles's disdain. But he needed Gilligan now, as became increasingly clear.

"We got to come up with a story to counter the facts they've dug up, Charles."

The kid to whom he'd given his ticket had happily told investigators in Denver what had happened in O'Hare. He had kept what was left of Charles's ticket as proof of the way he had conned a man out of a first class ticket with a story about his threatened engagement.

"You acted out of compassion," Gilligan said, trying it out. "But why did you take the shuttle back here?"

Several people on the shuttle had identified him, so much for his unrecorded return. Gilligan listened impassively while Charles told him again what had happened when he got home. He closed his eyes in thought and tried a possible reconstruction.

"Out of consideration for your wife, you didn't turn on any lights. You didn't want to wake her. We'll keep the part about stumbling too, that accounts for the furniture that was smashed up during the struggle.

"What struggle?"

Gilligan held up his hand. "Hey, I'm your lawyer. No bullshit, okay?"

Gilligan assumed he was guilty. His fate was sealed when Catherine decided to take the blame for what had happened. Charles was insanely jealous, she testified, and she and Fred had conspired to tease him. Fred Willis had pretended to be having an affair with Maud.

"I told Charles I knew they had been going to motels together."

Under oath, Gorman reluctantly admitted checking out motels for Charles. He had also taken around photographs of Maud and Fred.

"And?"

"Nothing."

"When I saw what it was doing to Charles," Catherine went on, looking tragically toward the jury, "I told Fred we had to stop. So I told Charles the big affair was all over. Maud had dismissed Fred."

Catherine burst into tears and Charles noted the sympathetic looks of the jurors. "It's all our fault. We drove him to it."

Despite Gilligan's best efforts, using what Catherine had said to play on the sympathy of the jurors, Charles got the maximum sentence from the woman judge who insisted in her instruction to the jury that when all was said and done this was a case of the cold blooded murder of a wife by a calculating, cruel husband who had no claim on their mercy.

"Fortunately he was stupid enough to leave unmistakable evidence of his foul deed. And he had the murder weapon in his hands when the police arrived."

Charles turned and looked at Fred Willis and his lying wife who was seated beside him. The gleam in Fred's eye before he turned away was that of guilt. Catherine had the look of a woman whose husband would be eternally in her debt. Charles was led away. He had lost both Maud and his freedom and there wasn't a soul in the world who would believe he was innocent. A more philosophical man might have considered that he was being punished for what he had intended to do. But, if he had been philosophical, he might have gotten used to Maud.

Miss Butterfingers

A Sister Mary Teresa Novella

1

By the second day, there was no doubt that the man was following her; he showed up in too many places for it to be a coincidence, but Kim let another day go by before she mentioned it to Joyce and Sister Mary Teresa.

"Tell him to knock it off," Joyce said, drawing on preconvent parlance. "Ignore him," Emtee Dempsey said. But Kim found it impossible to follow either bit of advice. Joyce offered to go with her, but it was hard to say what Joyce would do for several hours in the Northwestern library. And then suddenly one day there was the man, sitting in the reading room, looking about as comfortable as Joyce would have.

To feel compassion for a pest was not the reaction Kim expected from herself. Now after days of seeing that oval face, expressionless except for the eyes, whenever she turned around, she felt a little surge of pity.

She settled down to work, driving the man from her mind and was soon immersed in the research that, God and Sister Mary Teresa permitting, would eventually result in her doctoral dissertation. When she went to consult the card catalogue, she had completely forgotten her pursuer and when she turned to find herself face to face with him she let out an involuntary cry.

"Don't be frightened." He looked wildly around.

"I am not frightened. Why are you following me?"

He nodded. "I thought you'd noticed."

"What do you want?"

"I know you're a nun."

Well, that was a relief. The only indication in her dress that she was a religious was the veil she wore in the morning when the three of them went to the cathedral for Mass, but of course Kim didn't wear a veil on campus.

"Why not?" Sister Mary Teresa had asked. As far as the old nun was concerned the decision taken by the order to permit members either to retain the traditional habit, as Emtee Dempsey herself had done, or to wear such suitable dress as they chose was still in force, no matter that the three of them in the house on Walton Street were all that remained of the Order of Martha and Mary. The old nun was the superior of the house but would never have dreamt of imposing her personal will on the others. She had subtler ways of getting what she wanted. Of course, when it came to the rule, it was not a matter of imposing her will but that of their founder, Blessed Abigail Keineswegs, the authoress of the particular path to heaven they all had chosen when they were professed as nuns in the order.

"I think it has a negative effect on people."

"Perhaps a dissuasive effect is what a young woman your age might want from the veil, Sister."

"Oh for heaven's sake."

"Indeed."

The day Emtee Dempsey lost an argument would be entered in the Guinness Book of Records. What had been particularly annoying about the young man was the possibility that he did not know she was a nun and would ask for a date and then the explanation would be embarrassing. What a relief, accordingly, to learn that he knew her state in life.

"What is it you want?" She spoke with less aloofness. If he knew she was a nun, perhaps he was in some trouble and thought she might be of help.

"Oh, I don't want anything."

He looked intelligent enough; he was handsome in a way, dark hair, tall, nice smile lines around his eyes. Still, you never know. People with very low IQs don't always look it.

"You can't just follow people around. Would you want me to call a policeman?" The rag tag band of campus guards would not strike fear in many, but they looked like real policemen and as often as not that was enough.

"I am a policeman."

"You are!" Kim stepped back as if to get a better look at him. "Chicago or Evanston?"

"Chicago."

"I can check up on that, you know. What's your name?"

"Your brother doesn't know I've got this assignment. If you tell him, the whole point of it will be lost."

The allusion to Richard dispelled her skepticism. "What are you talking about?"

"There's been a threat against his family. You're part of his family."

"Who threatened him?"

"Does it matter? We're taking it seriously."

"But his wife and kids are the ones you should be looking after."

"We are."

"Nobody is going to harm me."

"I hope you're right. The reason I've been so obvious about following you is to let anyone who might try anything know that I'm around."

It seemed churlish to object to this and silly to ask how long it would continue.

"You didn't tell me your name."

"That's right." His grin was like a schoolboy's. Well, nuns brought out the boy in men; Kim had long been aware of that. Despite her age, she was often addressed as if she were the nun who had once rapped the knuckles of a now middle aged man. It wasn't necessary that she know her guardian's name, not if she couldn't call Richard and verify that he was a policeman.

After she knew why he was always around, his presence was more distracting rather than less. She felt self-conscious taking notes; every expression was one that might be observed. Within fifteen minutes, she closed her notebook and gathered up her things. All the way out to the Volkswagen bug and on the drive home to Walton Street, she assumed he was just behind her. Now that she knew he was following her, she couldn't find him. But at least she could tell Emtee Dempsey and Joyce what was going on.

"Oh, that's a relief," Joyce said sarcastically. "There's only a threat on your life and all along we thought it was something serious like a persistent Don Juan."

"He said Richard doesn't know?" Emtee Dempsey asked.

"That's right."

"But why wouldn't he be told? Why don't you call him?"

"What if our phone is tapped?"

Emtee Dempsey tried to look outraged but was actually delighted at the thought of such goings on. "And if we invite Richard to come over, the young man will of course assume you are going to tell him."

But Richard stopped by the next day unasked. He was ebullient and cheerful, turned down a beer twice before accepting one, sat in the study and looked around expansively.

"It's nice to stop by here when you're not interfering in my work."

"Richard, I have never interfered in your work," Sister Mary Teresa said primly.

His mouth opened in feigned shock and he looked apprehensively toward the ceiling. "I am waiting for a flash of lightning."

"I do not need dramatic divine confirmations of what I say."

"That isn't what I meant."

"What are you working on now?"

He shook his head. "Nothing important, but I would still rather not let you know."

"Very well. And how is your lovely family?"

"I think Agatha my oldest has a vocation."

"Really! What makes you think so?"

"No one can tell her a thing, she already knows it all."

"Richard!" Kim said.

He grinned. "Maybe it's just a stage she's going through."

"It must be very difficult for a child to have a father in the police force," the old nun said.

Richard's smile faded. "Why do you say that?"

"Oh, I don't know. Your work takes you among such unsavory elements. It must sometimes be difficult to protect your family from all that."

Kim gave Sister Mary Teresa a warning glance.

"I never bring my work home."

"Does it ever follow you there?"

"How do you mean?"

"Oh, I think of all the malefactors you have brought to justice. I imagine not all of them are grateful to you."

He laughed. "Sister, there are even some who resent it."

"That's my point."

"What is?"

Sister Mary Teresa hesitated. She had promised Kim she would not tell Richard that he and his family were being provided protection by his colleagues. She had come within an eyelash of saying it already and she was obviously trying to think what further she could say without breaking her promise.

"Who are some of your victims who might seek revenge?"

"Sister, if I worried about things like that I'd have entered a monastery rather than the department."

"Of course you wouldn't worry about it. I don't suggest that for a moment. Certainly not worry about your own safety. But just for the sake of conversation, if you had to pick someone who is in jail because of your efforts, blames you and might want to avenge himself, who would it be?"

Richard adopted the attitude of the man of the world telling a house of recluses what was going on outside their walls. Emtee Dempsey was fully prepared to play the naive innocent in order to keep Richard talking.

"The difficulty would be ruling anyone out," he said. "It's fairly routine for a crook after the verdict is in to turn and threaten any and every cop who was in on the investigation. This is especially true if you appear in court during the trial. Some even send letters once they're settled in at Joliet."

"Threats?"

"Kid stuff."

"But that's another crime, isn't it?"

"Sister, if we brought charges for every crime that's committed, I wouldn't be able to drop by for a social visit like this."

"You are a very evasive man, Richard."

"Thank you."

"You have managed not to name one single criminal who might actually seek to do you harm because you were instrumental in his arrest."

"I'll give you one."

"Good."

"Regina Fastnekker."

"The terrorist!"

"Miss Butterfingers."

Regina Fastnekker was the youngest daughter of a prominent Winnetka family whose fancy it was to be an anarchist. A modern political theory class at De Paul had convinced her that man and human society are fundamentally corrupt, reform is an illusion and the only constructive thing is to blow it all up. Something, Regina knew not what, would arise from the ashes, but whatever it was it could not be worse than the present situation and there was at least a chance it might be better. On the basis of a single chemistry class, Regina began to make explosives in the privacy of the apartment she rented in the Loop. Winnetka had become too irredeemable for her to bear to live with her parents any more. It was when one of her bombs went off, tearing out a wall and catapulting an upstairs neighbor into eternity, that Regina confessed to several bombings, one a public phone booth across the road from the entrance to Great Lakes Naval Base. When she was arrested, Regina's hair was singed nearly completely off and that grim bald likeness of her was something she blamed on Richard. In a corrupt world, Regina nonetheless wanted to look her best.

"You're part of the problem, cop," she shouted at him.

"Sure. That's why you're going to jail and I'm not."

"Someday," she said meaningfully.

"Some day what?"

"POW!"

Emtee Dempsey's eyes rounded as she listened. "How much longer will she be in jail?"

"How much longer? She was released after two years."

"When was that?"

"I don't know. A couple months ago."

"Richard, won't you have another beer?" Emtee Dempsey asked, pleased as punch. "I myself will have a cup of tea."

"Well, we can't have you drinking alone."

Having found out what she wanted, Emtee Dempsey chattered on about other things. It was Richard who returned to the subject of Miss Butterfingers.

"In court she screamed out her rage, threatening the judge, everyone, but when she pointed her finger at me, looking really demented, and vowed she'd get me, I felt a chill. I did. Nonetheless she was a model prisoner. Got religion. One of the Watergate penitents spoke at Joliet and she was among those who accepted Jesus as their personal savior."

"Then her punishment served her well."

"Yeah."

"Well, that cancels out Regina Fastnekker," Joyce said when Richard had gone.

"We could make a methodical check," Kim said.

"Or you could insist that your guardian angel tell you who has threatened Richard and his family. I should think you have a right to know if you have to put up with him wherever you go."

"I'll do it."

"I'm surprised you didn't insist on it when you talked with him."

Kim accepted the criticism, particularly since she was kicking herself for not finding out more from . . . But she hadn't even found out his name.

2

The next day two things happened that set the house on Walton Street on its ear, in Emtee Dempsey's phrase. At five in the morning, the house reverberated with a tremendous noise and they emerged from their rooms into the hallway, staring astounded at one another.

"What was that?" Joyce asked, her eyes looking like Orphan Annie's.

"An explosion."

As soon as Emtee Dempsey said it they realized that was indeed what they had heard. The old nun went back into her room and picked up the phone.

"It works," she said and put it down again. "Sister Kimberly, call the police."

Joyce said, "I'll check to see . . ."

"No." Emtee Dempsey hesitated. Then she went into Kim's room which looked out over Walton Street. They crowded around her. What looked to be pieces of their Volkswagen lay in the street, atop the roof of a red sedan and shredded upholstery festooned the power lines just below their eye level.

"Now you know what to report."

Kim picked up her own phone and made the call.

They were up and dressed when there was a ring at the door. Their call had not been necessary to bring the police. Emtee Dempsey was pensive throughout the preliminary inquiry, letting Kim answer most of the questions. At ten minutes of seven she stood.

"We must be off to Mass."

"Maybe you better not, Sister," Grimaldi said. He wore his salt and pepper hair cut short and his lids lay in diagonals across his eyes, giving him a sleepy friendly look.

"It is our practice to attend Mass every morning, Sergeant, and I certainly do not intend to alter it for this."

When he realized she was serious, he offered to drive them to the cathedral and Emtee Dempsey was about to refuse when the drama of arriving at St. Matthew's in a squad car struck her.

"Since we might otherwise be late, I agree. But no sirens."

He promised no sirens, thereby, Kim was sure, disappointing Emtee Dempsey.

It was, to put it mildly, a distracting way to begin the day. As it happened, their emergence from a police car at the cathedral door was witnessed by a derelict or two but otherwise caused no sensation. Once inside, Emtee Dempsey of course put aside such childishness. It was not until Richard joined Grimaldi that Emtee Dempsey brought up Miss Butterfingers. Richard squinted at her.

"All right, what's going on? How come you ask me about her yesterday and today your car's blown up?"

"Richard, you introduced her into the conversation. I may have asked a thing or two then, but if I ever heard of the young woman before I had forgotten it. Are you suggesting that she . . ."

"Aw, come on."

"Sergeant Grimaldi, has the lieutenant been told of the concern about him and his family?"

Grimaldi looked uncomprehending.

"Perhaps you weren't aware of it." She turned to Kim. "I think you will agree Sister that I am no longer bound by my promise."

"Of course not."

"Richard, your colleagues have been assigned to look after you and your family. Even Sister Kimberly has had an escort these past days."

Richard glared at Grimaldi, who lifted his shoulders. Richard then got on the phone. Emtee Dempsey's initial attitude was a little smug; clearly she enjoyed knowing something about the police that Richard did not know. But her manner changed as the meaning of Richard's end of the conversation became clear.

"There's been no protective detail assigned to my family. Where in hell did you get such a notion?"

Emtee Dempsey nodded to Kim.

"A man has been following me for several days. Two days ago I had enough and asked him what he was doing. He said he was a policeman."

"A Chicago policeman?"

"Yes."

"What's his name?"

"I don't know."

"Didn't you ask? Didn't you ask for his ID?"

"No, Richard. And I didn't call you up and ask what was going on either. At the time, I was relieved to learn why he was following me."

"Relieved that I was supposedly threatened?"

"Well, I was relieved to think that Mary and the kids . . ."

"I don't suppose he'll be following you around today," Richard broke in, "but I guarantee you a cop we know about will be."

"You want Sister to keep to her regular routine?"

"Sister Mary Teresa, I want all of you to follow your regular routines. And if anything relevant to this happens, I want to know about it pronto."

"An interesting use of the word, Richard. In Italian it means ready. It's how they answer the phone. Pronto," she said, trilling the R. "You on the other hand take it in its Spanish meaning."

There was more, much more, until Richard fled the study. At their much-delayed breakfast, the conversation was of the car. Joyce thought their insurance covered bombing. "Unless it's considered an act of God."

"Sister, a bombing is always an act of man. Or woman."

The newspaper lay on the table unattended throughout the meal. After all, the news of the day had happened in their street.

"I'll want to speak to Katherine about this. We don't want her to learn of it from the paper. What is in the paper, by the way?"

Joyce had taken the sports page and Kim, standing, was paging through the front section when she stopped and cried out. "That's him!"

"He," Emtee Dempsey corrected automatically, coming to stand beside her.

The picture was of a young man, smiling, confident, embarking on life. Perhaps a graduation photograph.

His name was Michael Layton. He had been found dead. He had been missing for five years. He was the man who identified himself as a policeman in the Northwestern library.

3

Katherine caught a cab and was in the house within half an hour of Emtee Dempsey's call, but of course there was far more to discuss now than the mere blowing up of their automobile. The street had been cordoned off, to the enormous aggravation and rage of who knows how many drivers, while special units collected debris and the all but intact rear end of the car, which seemed to have gone straight into the air, done a flip flop, and landed in their customary parking place.

"Dear God," Katherine Senski said. "They might be out there collecting pieces of you three."

"Nonsense," Emtee Dempsey said.

A first discovery was that the device had not been one that would have been triggered by starting the car. This conclusion was reached by noting the intact condition of the rear of the car.

"But aren't such devices hooked up to starters, to motors?"

"The motor was in the rear end," Joyce explained.

"Oh," Katherine said, but the three nuns were suddenly struck by that past tense. Their Volkswagen bug was no more.

They had just settled down at the dining room table with a fresh pot of coffee when Benjamin Rush arrived. The elegant lawyer stood in the doorway, taking in the scene, and then resumed his usual air of unruffled savoir-faire.

"It is a relief to see you, as the saying goes, in one piece, Sister. Sisters."

They made room for him, but of course he refused coffee. He had had the single cup that must make do until lunchtime. Joyce brought him a glass of mineral water, which he regarded ruefully, not interrupting Emtee Dempsey's colorful account of Kim's being followed, her confronting the man, their attempt to get information from Richard. And then this morning. By the time she got to the actual explosion, it might have been wondered how she could keep the dramatic line of her narrative rising, so exciting the preliminary events were made to sound. Kim found herself wishing she had actually behaved with the forthrightness Emtee Dempsey attributed to her when she confronted her supposed police escort in the Northwestern library. Emtee Dempsey had the folded morning paper safely under one pudgy hand, clearly her prop for the ultimate revelation. But there was so much to be said before she got to it.

"Regina Fastnekker! Do I remember that one," Katherine said. "My pre-trial interviews?" She looked around the table. "I was nominated for a Pulitzer, for heaven's sake."

"Do you still have them?"

Katherine smiled sweetly. "My scrapbooks are up to date, thank you."

Benjamin Rush wanted to know where Regina was now. Katherine, to her shame, had not followed further the Fastnekker saga once the girl had been safely put away. Emtee Dempsey told them of the woman's supposed prison conversion.

"Supposed in the sense of alleged. I do not mean to express skepticism. Some of the greatest saints got their start in prison."

"I won't ask you how many lawyers have been canonized," Mr. Rush said and sipped his mineral water.

Katherine said, "Conversion isn't a strong enough word for the turn around that girl would have needed. I have seldom talked with anyone I considered so, well, diabolic. She seemed to have embraced evil."

"Evil be thou my good," murmured Emtee Dempsey.

"Who said that?"

"Milton's Satan, of course, don't tease. I must read every word you wrote about her, Katherine. I suppose the police will know where she is to be found."

"I suspect they may be talking with her right now."

"The bombing is in her style," Rush said. "Ominously so. It is why I came directly here. Katherine will know better than I that the Fastnekker crowd had a quite unique modus operandi. There was always a series of bombings, the first a kind of announcement, defiant, and then came the big bang. What

I am saying is that, far from being out of danger, you may be in far more danger now than before the unfortunate destruction of your means of transportation. If, that is, we are truly dealing with Regina Fastnekker and company."

"Company? How many were there?"

"It's all in my stories," Katherine said. "I wonder why I didn't read of her big conversion."

"If it is genuine, she might not have wanted it to be a media event."

"Well, you have certainly had some morning. But, as Benjamin says, the excitement may be just beginning. I suggest that you go at once to the lake place in Indiana."

"No, no, no," Rush intervened. He thought that for them to be in such a remote place, where the police were, well, local, far from taking the nuns out of danger might well expose them fatally.

"We have to assume that you are being watched at this very moment."

"Isn't it far more likely that the next attempt will be on Richard's family?"

Katherine said, "I wonder who that phony policeman was?"

That was Emtee Dempsey's cue. "I was coming to that," she said, unfolding the paper. "This is the man."

"But that's Michael Layton," Mr. Rush said in shocked tones.

"Ah, you know him."

"Sister, that boy, that young man, disappeared several years ago. Vanished into thin air."

"That's in the story, Benjamin."

"But I know the Laytons. I knew Michael. I can't tell you what a traumatic experience it was for them."

Emtee Dempsey turned to Katherine. "Was this young

man part of Regina Fastnekker's company?"

"That's not possible," said Mr. Rush.

"Why on earth would he impersonate a policeman?"

"Sister Kimberly, please call your brother and tell him that Michael Layton was the one following you around of late."

It was Katherine who summed it all up; despite the evident pain it caused Benjamin Rush. Alerted by what the young man following Sister Kimberly had said, Emtee Dempsey had coaxed from Richard his belief that Regina Fastnekker was more likely than anyone else to seek to do him harm after she was released from jail. She had masked her intention by undergoing a religious conversion while in prison and some time had elapsed since she had regained her freedom. Richard himself had been lulled into the belief that Miss Butterfingers had gotten over her desire for revenge. She chose to strike where it would be least expected, at Richard's sister. Accordingly, one of the gang followed Kim around and, when confronted, disarmingly claimed to be part of a police effort to protect Richard's family. This morning, their automobile was blown up, a typical first move in the Fastnekker modus operandi.

By this point in Katherine's explanation, Emtee Dempsey had plunged her face into her hands. But Benjamin Rush took it up.

"Michael was then killed for warning Sister Kimberly that she was in danger." The lawyer's spirit rose at the thought of his friends' son exhibiting his natural goodness at such peril to his life.

"What a tissue of conjecture," Emtee Dempsey observed, looking around at her friends. "In the first place, we have no reason at all to think that Michael Layton was connected with this Fastnekker terrorist gang."

"Of course we don't," Benjamin Rush said, switching field.

"Nor do we have any reason to think this is the work of the Fastnekker gang. The idea that her religious conversion was a ploy must deal with the fact that she tried to keep it quiet."

"The sneakiest publicity of all," Joyce said.

"Salinger," Kim agreed.

"What?" Emtee Dempsey looked at her two young colleagues as if they had lost their minds. But she waved away whatever it was they referred to. "We know only two things. First, that a young man named Michael Layton, who has been missing for years, who was lately following Sister Kimberly and claimed to be a policeman when she spoke to him, is dead. Second, we know that our automobile has been destroyed."

"Our insurance company will probably suspect us of that," Joyce said.

Benjamin Rush rose. "You are absolutely right, Sister. I have entered into this speculative conversation but I must repeat that I cannot believe Michael Layton could possibly be involved in anything wrong or criminal. Let us hope that the police will be able to cast light on what has happened."

4

It was not only those on Walton Street who were reminded of the Fastnekker gang by the exploding Volkswagen. An editorial in the rival of Katherine's paper expressed the hope that Chicago and indeed the country was not on the threshold of a renewal of the terrorism of a decade ago. Readers were reminded of the various groups, including that led by Regina Fastnekker and the fear was stated that the destruction of the car was only a prelude to something worse. How many, like the unfortunate Michael Layton, products of good homes, having all the advantages of American society, suddenly dropped from sight only to turn up, incredibly, as terrorists? The editorial immediately added that there was absolutely no evidence of any connection of Layton with any terrorist efforts, though the explanation he had given of following a member of a Chicago policeman's family would doubtless prompt some to make that connection. Lieutenant Richard Moriarity had led the investigation that resulted in the successful prosecution of Regina Fastnekker.

Katherine Senski threw the paper down on Emtee Dempsey's desk and fell into a chair. "That is completely and absolutely irresponsible. It is one thing to sit among friends and try to tie things together, but to publish such random thoughts in a supposedly respectable newspaper, well . . ." She threw up her hands, at a loss for words.

But Katherine's reaction was nothing to that of Benjamin Rush. Below his distinguished snow-white hair, his patrician features were rosy with rage.

"It is an outrageous accusation against a man who cannot defend himself."

"Perhaps the Layton family will sue."

"I am on my way there now. That is precisely what they want to do. Alas, I shall advise them not to. The editorial cunningly fends off the accusation of libel by qualifying or seeming to take back what it had just said. When you add the first amendment, there simply is no case. Legally. Morally, whoever wrote this is a scoundrel. I now understand the feelings of clients who have urged me to embark on a course I knew could end only in failure. One wants to tilt at windmills!"

"You will be talking to the Laytons today?"

An immaculate cuff appeared from the sleeve of Benjamin

Rush's navy blue suit as he lifted his arm and then a watch whose unostentatiousness was in a way ostentatious came into view. "In half an hour. I have come to ask you a favor. Actually, to ask Sister Kimberly."

"Anything," Kim said. No member of the Order of Martha and Mary could be unaware of their debt to Benjamin Rush. He had saved this house at the time of the great dissolution and had insured that an endowment would enable the order to continue in however reduced a form.

"It would be particularly consoling for the Laytons if they could speak to someone who saw Michael as recently as you have."

The request made Kim uneasy. What if the Laytons wished to derive consolation from the fact that it was a nun who had spoken to their son? Kim herself had wondered if he had not perhaps thought that she could be of help, directly or indirectly, in some difficulty.

"I should tell you that while Melissa Layton is quite devout, her husband Geoffrey is a member of the Humanist Society and regards all religion as a blight."

"Find out which of them the son favored, Sister."

Having already agreed to help Mr. Rush, there was nothing Kim could do, but she was profoundly unwilling to talk to grieving parents about a son they had not seen in years and to whom she had spoken once, in somewhat odd circumstances. Mr. Rush's car stood at the curb where the Volkswagen had always been, but the contrast could not have been greater. Long and gray with tinted glass it seemed to require several spaces. Marvin, Mr. Rush's chunky driver, opened the door and Kim got in, with Mr. Rush at seemingly the opposite end of a sofa. They drove off in comfort to the Laytons.

On the way, Mr. Rush told her a few more things about the Laytons, but nothing could have prepared her adequately for the next several hours. Kim had somehow gotten the impression that the Laytons would be Mr. Rush's age, which was foolish when she considered that the son had been closer to her age, but Mrs. Layton was a shock. She was beautiful, her auburn hair worn shoulder length, her face as smooth as a girl's and the black and silver housecoat, floor length, billowed about her, heightening the effect she made as she crossed the room to them. Kim felt dowdy in her sensible suit, white blouse and veil and it didn't help to remind her that her costume befitted her vocation. Melissa Layton tipped her cheek for Mr. Rush's kiss and extended a much braceleted arm to Kim.

"Sister." Both hands enclosed Kim's and her violet eyes scanned Kim's face. "Ben assured us that you would come."

Geoffrey Layton rose from his chair, nodded to Rush and gave a little bow to Kim but his eyes were fastened on her veil.

"Come," Mrs. Layton said. She had not released Kim's hand and led her to a settee where they could sit side by side. "Tell me of your meeting with Michael." And suddenly the beauty was wrenched into sorrow and the woman began to sob helplessly. Now Kim held her hand. Mrs. Layton's tears made Kim feel a good deal more comfortable in this vast room with its period furniture, large framed pictures and magnificent view.

Mrs. Layton emerged from her bout of grief even more beautiful than before, tear drops glistening in her eyes, but composed. Mr. Layton and Mr. Rush stood in front of the seated woman while Kim told her story.

"How long had he been following you around?"

"For several days."

"That you know of," Mrs. Layton said.

"Yes. I spoke of it with the other sisters. At first it was just a nuisance but then it became disturbing. We decided that I should talk to him. On Wednesday morning . . ."

"Wednesday," Mrs. Layton repeated, and her expression suggested she was trying to remember what she had been doing at the time this young woman beside her had actually spoken to her long lost son. "He said he knew I was a nun."

"Of course," said Mr. Layton.

"I do not wear my veil when I go to Northwestern."

"Why not?"

"I just don't."

"Could he have seen you with it on?"

"I suppose."

"But what did he say?" Mrs. Layton asked. Kim was aware that another woman had come into the room, her hair and coloring the same as Mrs. Layton's, though without the dramatic beauty. Mrs. Layton turned to see what Kim was looking at. "Janet, come here. This is Sister Kimberly who talked with your brother Michael."

The daughter halved the distance between them but as Kim talked on, answering questions that became more and more impossible, about the Layton son, Janet came closer. The parents wanted to know what he looked like, how he acted, did she think he was suffering from amnesia, on and on, and from time to time when Kim glanced at Janet she got a look of sympathy. Finally the younger woman stepped past Mr. Rush.

"Thank you so much for telling us about your meeting with Michael."

Comparing the two women, Kim could now see that, youthful as Mrs. Layton looked, she looked clearly older than her daughter who made no effort to be attractive.

The Laytons now turned to Mr. Rush to insist that he bring suit against the editorialist who had slandered their son. Janet led Kim away.

"There's coffee in the kitchen."

"Oh good."

"You realize that all this is to put off the evil day. We have not seen Michael's body. It is a question whether we will. As a family. I certainly intend to."

There was both strength and genuineness in Janet Layton and, Kim could see, when they were sitting on stools in the kitchen, sipping coffee, that with the least of efforts Janet could rival her mother in beauty. If she didn't it was because she felt no desire to conceal her mourning.

"You're a nun?"

"Yes."

"I wanted to be a nun once. I suppose most girls think of it."

"Very briefly."

"What's it like?"

"Come visit us. We have a house on Walton Street."

"Near the Newberry?"

"Just blocks away. Do you go there?"

She nodded. "What is so weird is that I also use the Northwestern library. What if I had gone there Wednesday?"

"I hope I made it clear that your brother seemed perfectly all right to me. But then I thought he was the policeman he said he was and that changed everything. He looked the part."

"It's cruel after years of thinking him dead to find out he was alive on Wednesday, in a place I go to, but now is truly dead." Her lip trembled and she looked away.

"He just disappeared?"

She nodded, not trusting herself to speak for a moment. "One day he left the house for school and never came back. No note, no indication he was going; he took nothing with him. He just ceased to exist, or so it seemed. The police searched, my parents hired private investigators. My father, taking the worst thing he could think of, suspected the Moonies. But not one single trace was found."

"On his way to school?"

"Chicago. He was an economics major."

"How awful."

"I don't know how my parents bore up under this. My mother of course never lets herself go physically, but inside she has been devastated. It is the first time my father confronted something he couldn't do anything effective about. That shook him almost as much as the loss of Michael."

"Mr. Rush says your mother is very devout."

"Let me show you something."

They went rapidly through the house that was far larger than Kim's first impression of it. On an upper floor as they came down a hallway stood a small altar. There was a statue of perhaps three feet in height of Our Blessed Lady and a very large candle in a wrought iron holder burning before it. Janet turned and widened her eyes significantly as she indicated the shrine.

"Mother's. For the return of her lost son."

There was nothing to say to that. Janet went into a room and waited for Kim to join her.

"This is just the way it was when he disappeared. Michael's room. Maybe now mother will agree to . . ."

No need to develop the thought. No doubt Mrs. Layton would consider it an irreverence to get rid of her son's clothes and other effects, even though she knew now he was dead. A computer stood on the desk, covered with a clear plastic hood. A bookshelf, the top row of which contained works in or related to economics. The other shelves were a hodgepodge, largely paperbacks, mysteries, westerns, science fiction, classics. Michael Layton had either unsettled literary tastes or universal interests.

"The police checked over this room and the private investigators Daddy hired also looked it over. They found no indication Mike intended to leave and of course that introduced a note of hope. That he'd been kidnapped, for instance. But no demands were made. Every investigation left us where we'd been—with something that made utterly no sense."

"It must have been awful."

"I am glad the waiting is over, after all these years. Does that sound terrible?"

"No."

"I wanted you to see this. I wanted you to know that there are no clues here."

Kim smiled. "You've heard of Sister Mary Teresa?"

Janet nodded.

As they went downstairs, Kim reflected that if Janet was right, and why wouldn't she be, the explanation for Michael Layton's murder would have to be sought in what he had been doing in the years since he left his home for the last time. And no one seemed to know where on earth he had been.

5

"Miss Butterfingers is going to call on us," Joyce whispered when Kim returned to Walton Street.

"Wow."

"Just what I said to Emtee Dempsey."

"Yes," Sister Mary Teresa said, when Kim went into the study and asked about the impending visit. "Miss Fastnekker called half an hour ago and asked if she might come by. I am trying to read these articles of Katherine's before our visitor arrives. Here are the ones I've read." Kim took the photocopies and began to read them as she crossed to a chair. What a delight they were. This was Katherine at the height of her powers, the woman who had been the queen of Chicago journalism longer than it was polite to mention. Reading those old stories acquainted Kim with the kind of person she preferred not to know. The Regina Fastnekker Katherine had interviewed intensively and written about with rare evocative power was a prophet of doom, an angel of destruction, a righteous scourge of mankind. At twenty-two years old, she had concluded that human beings are hopelessly corrupt, there is nothing to redeem what is laughingly called civilization. Any judgment that what she had done was illegal or immoral proceeded from a system so corrupt as to render such charges comic. Katherine described Regina as a nihilist, one who preferred nothing to everything that was. It was not that the world had this or that flaw, the world was the flaw.

"I am glad you don't have possession of hydrogen weapons," Katherine had observed.

"Atomic destruction is the solution. Inevitably one day it will arrive. I have been anticipating that awful self-judgment of mankind on itself by the actions I have taken."

"Who appointed you to this destructive task?"

"I did."

"Have you ever doubted your judgment?"

"Not on these matters."

"From the point of view of society, it makes sense to lock you up, wouldn't you say?"

"Society will regret what has been done to me."

Katherine had clearly been as awed as Kim was now that a woman who had done such deeds, who had killed by accident rather than design, should continue to speak with such conviction that she was somehow not implicated in the universal guilt of the race to which she belonged.

"You are employing a corrupt logic," Miss Butterfingers had replied.

Katherine had concluded that the only meaning "corrupt" seemed to have was "differing from Regina Fastnekker."

"What a sweetheart," Kim commented when she had finished.

"We must not forget that this was the Regina of some years ago. On the phone she seemed very nice."

"Did you tell her the police would know if she visited us?"

"I saw no reason to say such a thing."

Emtee Dempsey had invited Regina to come to Walton Street on the assumption that she was now a changed woman, radically different from the terrorist so graphically portrayed by Katherine Senski in her newspaper series. If she was wrong, if Regina had been behind the blowing up of the Volkswagen and if her custom was to announce a serious deed by a lesser one, Emtee Dempsey could be inviting their assassin to visit. She did not have to wonder what Richard would say if asked about the advisability of admitting Regina to their home.

The woman who stood at the door when Kim went to answer the bell wore a denim skirt that reached her ankles and an oversize cable knit sweater; her hair was pulled back severely on her head and held with a rubber band. Pale blue eyes stared unblinkingly at Kim.

"I have come to see Sister Dempsey."

There was no mistaking that this was Regina Fastnekker, despite the changes that had occurred in her since the photos that accompanied Katherine's stories. Kim opened the door and took Regina down the hall to the study. Her back tingled as she walked as if she awaited some unexpected blow to fall. But she made it to the study door without incident.

"Sister Mary Teresa, this is Regina Fastnekker."

The old nun did not rise but watched closely as her guest came to the desk. Regina put out her hand and the old nun stood as she took it.

"Welcome to our home."

"I must tell you that I consider the Catholic Church to be the corruption of Christianity and that it is only by a return to the gospels that we can be saved. One person at a time."

"Ecclesia semper reformanda."

"I don't understand."

"You express a sentiment as old as Christianity itself. Do you know the story of the order St. Francis founded?"

"St. Francis is someone I admire."

"I was sure you would. Francis preached holy poverty, personifying it, calling it Lady Poverty, his beloved. After his death, his followers disputed what this meant. Could they for example own a house and live in it, or did poverty require them to own absolutely nothing and rely each day on the Lord to provide? Did they own the clothes they wore, since of course each one wore his own clothes?"

"Why are you telling me this?"

"It is possible to make Christianity so pure that it ceases to be."

"It is also possible to falsify it so much that it ceases to be."

"Of course."

"You sound as if you had won an argument."

"I wasn't aware we were having one. I am told that you have become a Christian."

"That makes it sound like something I did. It was done to me. It is a grace of which I am entirely unworthy."

"Do you know Michael Layton?"

The sudden switch seemed to surprise Regina. She rearranged her skirt, and pushed up the sleeve of her sweater.

"I knew him."

"Before your conversion?"

"Before I went to prison, yes."

"Have you seen him since?"

"I came here to tell you that I have not."

"Have you any idea who killed him?"

"That is the question the police put to me in a dozen different ways."

"And how did you answer?"

"Yes and no."

"How yes?"

"I saw his photograph in the paper."

"Ah."

"It is my intention always to tell the truth, even when it seems trivial."

"An admirable ideal. It is one I share."

There was not a trace of irony in Emtee Dempsey's tone, doubtless because she felt none. Her ability to speak so that she did not technically tell a lie, however much others might mislead themselves when listening to her, was something Kim tried not to be shocked at. Whenever they discussed the matter, the old nun's defense—if it could even be called a defense—was unanswerable but Kim in her heart of hearts felt that Emtee Dempsey should be a good deal more candid than she was.

"The truth, the whole truth, and nothing but the truth," she had reminded the old nun.

"A noble if empty phrase."

"Empty?"

"What is the whole truth about the present moment? Only God knows. I use the phrase literally. Since we cannot know the whole truth we cannot speak it."

"We can speak the whole truth that we know."

"Alas, that too is beyond our powers. Even as we speak,

what we know expands and increases and we shall never catch up with it."

"You know what I mean."

"Only by what you say, my dear, and I am afraid that does not make much sense."

"I didn't invent the phrase."

You have at least that defense."

But now, speaking to Regina Fastnekker, Emtee Dempsey seemed to be suggesting that she herself sought always to tell the whole truth. If they were alone, Kim might have called her on this. But at the moment, she watched with fascination the alertness with which Regina listened to the old nun. In her articles, Katherine had described the ingenue expression Regina wore when she pronounced her nihilistic doctrines. Her beliefs might have changed, but her expression had not. Now she looked out at the world with the innocence of one who had been saved by religious conversion, but nonetheless, however much she had changed, Regina Fastnekker was still on the side of saved.

"What I have come to tell you is that I did not blow up your car, and I have no intention to harm you."

"I am glad to hear that."

"I tell you because it would be reasonable to think I had, given my sinful past. I am still a sinner, of course, but I have chosen Jesus for my personal savior and have with the help of his grace put behind me such deeds."

"You have been blessed."

"So have you. If I had not been converted I might very well have conceived such a scheme and put it into operation."

"And killed me?"

"The loved ones of those who put me in prison."

"A dreadful thought."

Regina said nothing for a moment and when she spoke it

was with great deliberateness. "I have never killed anyone. I do not say this to make myself seem less terrible than I was. But I never took another's life."

"I had thought someone died when an explosion occurred in your apartment."

"That is true."

"And you were the cause of that explosion."

"No. It was an accident."

"You express yourself with a great deal of precision."

"Praise the Lord."

Seldom had the phrase been spoken with less intonation. Regina put her hands on her knees and then rose in an almost stately manner.

"I challenge you to accept the Lord as your savior."

"My dear young lady, I took the vows of religion nearly fifty years ago. I took Jesus as my spiritual spouse, promising poverty, chastity and obedience. But I take your suggestion in good grace and shall endeavor to follow your advice."

Regina Fastnekker, apparently having no truth, however trivial to utter, said nothing. She bowed and Kim took her to the door.

"Thank you for visiting us."

"Did you too take those vows?"

"Yes. But not fifty years ago."

Regina Fastnekker's smile was all the more brilliant for being so rare. Her laughter had a pure soprano quality. Lithe, long-limbed, her full skirt lending a peculiar dignity to her passage, she went across the porch, descended the steps and disappeared up the walk.

6

Two days later, in the Northwestern University library, Kim looked up from the book she was reading to find Janet Layton smiling down on her.

"Can we talk?" she whispered.

Kim, startled to see the sister where she had had such a dramatic encounter with the brother, got up immediately. Outside, Janet lit up a cigarette.

"There is something I should have told you the other day and didn't. In fact I lied to you. I have known all along that Mike was still alive."

"You did!"

"He telephoned me in my dorm room within a month of his disappearance. The first thing he said was that he did not want my parents to know of the call."

"And you agreed?"

"I didn't tell them. I don't think I would have in any case. You would have to know how terribly they took Mike's disappearance, particularly at the beginning. If I had told them, they would have wanted proof. There was none I could give. And of course I had no idea then that it would turn into a permanent disappearance. I don't know that he himself thought so at the time."

"What did he want?"

"He wanted some computer disks from his room."

She had complied, putting the disks in a plastic bag and the bag in a trash container on a downtown Chicago corner. She walked away, as she had been instructed, but with the idea of hiding and watching the container. She took up her station inside a bookstore and watched the container. Clerks asked if they could be of help and she shook her head, her eye never leaving the container. After an hour, the manager came and she moved to a drugstore, certain her eyes had never left the container. After four hours of vigil, she was out of patience. She decided to take the disks from the container and wait for another phone call from her brother. The plastic bag containing the disks was gone.

"I felt like a bag lady, rummaging around in that trash, people turning to look at me. But it was definitely gone. Someone must have taken it within minutes of my putting it there, while I was walking away."

"And your brother called again?"

"Months later. I asked him if he got the disks. He said yes. That was all. His manner made me glad I'd done what I had."

Before leaving the disks in the container, Janet had made copies of them. She opened her purse and took out a package.

"Would you give these to Sister Mary Teresa?"

"You should give them to the police."

"I will leave that up to her. If that's what she thinks should be done with them, all right."

"Did you read the disks?"

"I tried to once. I don't know what program they're written on, but I typed them out at the DOS prompt. They looked like notes on reading to me. The fact that Mike wanted them means only that they were important to him. Frankly, I'd rather not admit that I've heard from Mike over the years. My parents would never understand my silence."

Kim had difficulty understanding it herself. Emtee Dempsey on the other hand found it unsurprising.

"But of course it would have been unsurprising if she told them too. Singular choices do not always have moral necessity. There were doubtless good reasons for either course of action and she chose the one she did."

"What will you do with them?"

"What the young lady suggested. Study their contents. Can you print them out for me?"

Before she did anything with the disk, Kim took the same precaution Janet had and made copies of them. There were three disks, of the five and a half inch size, but only two were full, the third had only 12,000 bytes saved on it. Running a directory on them, Kim jotted down the file names.

BG&E.one

BG&E.two

TSZ.one

TSZ.two

TSZ.tre

That was the contents of the first disk. The second was similarly uninformative.

PENSEES.UNO

PENSEES.DOS

PENSEES.TRE

The third disk had one file, AAV.

The files had not been written on Notabene, the program Kim preferred, nor on either Word or Wordperfect. Kim printed them from ASCI and began reading eagerly as they emerged from the printer but quickly, as Janet had, found her interest flag. Michael Layton seemed to have devised a very personal kind of shorthand. "Para fn eth no es vrd, pero an attmpt para vanqr los grnds."

Let Emtee Dempsey decipher that if she could. The fact that Michael Layton wrote in a way difficult if not impossible to follow suggested that the disks contained information of interest. The old nun spread the sheets before her, smoothing them out, a look of anticipation on her pudgy face. Kim left her to her task.

The old nun was preoccupied at table and after night prayers returned to her study. At one in the morning, Kim came downstairs to find Emtee Dempsey brooding over the printout. She looked up at Kim and blinked.

"Any luck?"

"You are right to think that decoding always depends on finding one little key. Whether it is a matter of luck, I do not know."

"Have you found the key?"

"No."

"I couldn't make heads nor tails of it."

"Oh, the first two disks present no problem. They are paraphrases of Nietzsche."

"You mean you can understand those pages?"

"Only to the degree that Nietzsche himself is intelligible. The young man paraphrased passages from the mad philosopher and interspersed his own comments, most of them jejune."

"How did you know it was Nietzsche?"

"Beyond Good and Evil. Thus Spake Zarathustra."

"And the second is Pascal?"

"Unfortunately, no. The thoughts are young Layton's, thoughts of unrelieved tedium and banality. Do you know the Pensieri of Leopardi? Giacomo Leopardi?"

"I don't even know who he is."

"Was. His work of that name is a collection of pessimistic and misanthropic jottings, puerile, adolescent. If a poet of genius, however troubled, was capable of writing such silliness, we should not perhaps be too harsh with young Layton."

"What is on the third disk?"

She shook her head. "Those few pages are written in a bad imitation of *Finnegan's Wake*, a kind of macaronic relying on a variety of languages imperfectly understood. I had hoped that the first disks would provide me with the clue needed to understand the third, but so far this is . . ."

An explosion shook the house, bringing Emtee Dempsey to her feet. But Kim was down the hall ahead of her and dashed upstairs. As she came into the upstairs hall, she saw that a portion of the left wall as well as her door had been blown away. The startled face of Joyce appeared through plaster cloud.

"Strike two," she said.

7

Sister Mary Teresa wanted to take a good look around Kim's room before calling the police, although why the neighborhood had failed to be shaken awake by the explosion was explained by the incessant street racket that did not really cease until three or sometimes four in the morning. The explosion of Kim's computer would have been only one noise among many to those outside, however it had filled the house. The wall that had been blown into the hall was the one against which Kim's computer had stood.

"Why would it do a thing like that?" the old nun asked.

"I've never heard of it before."

"Was it on?"

"I never turn it off." Kim explained the theory behind this.

They puzzled over the event for perhaps fifteen minutes before Kim called Richard, relying on him to alert the appropriate experts. They came immediately, a tall woman with flying straight hair and her companion whose thick glasses seemed to have become part of his face. They picked around among the debris, eyes bright with interest. This was something new to them as well.

"Computers don't blow up," the girl said.

"There had to be a bomb." Behind the thick lenses

her companion's eyes widened.

"When did you last use the machine?"

"I printed out some disks."

"Any sign of them?"

They were in the plastic box that had bounced off the far wall and landed on her bed. She opened it and showed them the five disks it contained.

"Five!" she exclaimed. "There are only five."

"Only?"

She showed them the three copies she had made, and two of the discs she had been given by Janet Layton. And then she remembered. "I left the third in the drive."

"Can a computer disk be a bomb?" Emtee Dempsey asked.

Her question brought amused smiles to the two experts. The girl said, "Anything can be a bomb."

"Michael Layton delivered his second bomb," Emtee Dempsey said. "Posthumously."

"Janet Layton gave them to me," Kim reminded her.

"Yes. Yes, she did."

Richard came and kept them up until three going over what had happened. Kim let Emtee Dempsey tell the story she herself had heard from Janet Layton. She went over in her mind the conversation she had had with Janet at the Layton home and then what she had said at Northwestern that afternoon. If Janet had told her the truth, the disks she had given Kim were copies of those her brother made, rather than his originals. If one of those disks had been made into a bomb, it had to have been by Janet. But why?

"I'll ask her why. And I don't intend to wait for daylight either."

The next time Kim saw Janet Layton was under police

auspices. The violet eyes widened when Kim came in.

"Oh."

"I'm alive."

"Thank God."

She rose and reached a hand across the table. Mastering her aversion, Kim took the hand. Janet turned to Richard.

"Why didn't you tell me she was unharmed?"

"I don't talk to people who don't talk to me."

Janet talked now. What she had told Kim was true as far as it went, well, almost. She had not, years ago, made copies of the disks her brother asked her to bring, but everything else had happened as it had.

"Regina told me to tell you what I did."

"Regina Fastnekker!"

Janet nodded. "After Michael's death, she called me. She asked me if I remembered delivering some computer disks to Michael long ago. Of course I did. She said she had them and felt they might help solve the mystery of Michael's death. She asked if I would pass them on to you with just the message I gave you. You could decide, or Sister Mary Teresa could decide, what to do with them."

Richard made a face. "She knew she could rely on the nosiness of you know who."

But he was on his feet and heading out of the room. "I'm going to let you go," he said to Janet.

"Come with me," Kim said. There was no substitute for Emtee Dempsey's hearing this story from Janet herself.

But the old nun merely nodded impatiently as Janet spoke. Her interest was entirely in Regina Fastnekker. Katherine, having heard of the second explosion on Walton Street, hurried over but Janet stayed on, far from being the center of attention. Katherine was almost triumphant when she heard the news that the supposedly converted Regina Fastnekker had used Janet to deliver a second bomb to Walton Street.

"The brazen thing," she fumed, a grim smile on her face.

"You think she blew up our car?"

"Of course. Your car, Michael Layton and very nearly Sister Kimberly. Oh, I never believe these stories of radical conversion. People just don't change character that easily."

"She denied it, Katherine."

"It's part of her new persona. But the gall of the woman, to use the same pattern she always used before."

"As if she were drawing attention to herself."

"More insolence," Katherine said.

Regina Fastnekker denied quite calmly through hours of interrogation that she had killed anybody. Richard, when he brought this news to Walton Street, regarded it as just what one would expect.

"But she does talk to you?"

"Talk?" He shook his head. "She goes on and on, like a TV preacher. How she has promised the Lord to tell the truth and that is what she is doing."

"I suppose you have gone over the place where Regina lives?"

Richard nodded. "Nothing."

"And this does not shake your confidence that she is responsible for these bombings?"

"You know what I think? I think she sat in prison all those years and planned this down to the minute. But she wasn't going to risk being sent to prison again. She would do it and do it in a way that I would know she had done it and yet would not be able to prove she had."

"Can you?"

"We will. We will."

Katherine wrote a feature on the "Backsliding Miss Butterfingers," in the words of the header. The veteran reporter permitted herself some uncharacteristic forays into what made someone like Regina Fastnekker tick. Prison may not breed criminals, her argument ran, but it receives a criminal and releases him or her worse than he or she was before.

"Wouldn't 'he' be sufficient?"

"I've told you of our manual of style?"

"Style is the man," Emtee Dempsey purred. "Would you be allowed to write that?"

Katherine seemed to be blushing beneath her powdered cheeks. " 'Style is the woman' is the way it will appear in my tomorrow's article."

"Et tu, Katherine? Didn't Regina take credit for what she had done when she was arrested before?"

"She did."

"And now she continues to deny what she is accused of?"

" 'I have not touched a bomb since I left prison.' That's it verbatim."

"Gloves?"

"I thought of that. Something in the careful way she speaks suggested that I do. 'As far as I know I have never been in the vicinity of an explosive device since leaving prison.' "

"What does she say about what Janet Layton told us?"

"She denies it."

"How?"

"She says it is a lie."

"Verbatim?"

"Verbatim."

"Hmmm."

The following morning when they were returning from St. Matthews, on foot, creating a sensation, Emtee Dempsey suddenly stopped and clapped her hands.

"Of course!" she cried, and began to laugh. When she set

off again, it was almost skippingly, and her great starched headdress waggled and shook. Joyce and Kim exchanged a look. The mind is a delicate thing.

Emtee Dempsey bounded up the porch steps and inside removed the shawl from her shoulders.

"First breakfast, then call Richard."

"Why not ask him for breakfast?" Joyce said facetiously.

"No. Afterward. Let's try for ten o'clock and we want everyone here. The Laytons, Katherine, Regina Fastnekker and of course Richard."

"Regina Fastnekker is under arrest."

"That is why we must convey the invitation through Richard."

"He is not going to bring a mad bomber to the scene of the crime."

"Nonsense. I'll talk to him if necessary."

"I'll talk to her," Richard said, "but it's not necessary, it's impossible, as in it necessarily can't happen. I am not going to help her put on one of her amateur theatricals."

"You have every reason to object," Emtee Dempsey said, already on the phone in her study. "But wouldn't you like to clear this matter up?"

"Only what is obscure can be cleared up. This is simple as sin. We have the one responsible for those bombings."

"There's where you are wrong, Richard."

"How in hell can you know that?"

"The provenance of my knowledge is elsewhere. I realized what had happened when we were returning from Mass less than an hour ago."

"Not on your life, Sister Mary Teresa. And I mean it."

With that outburst, Kim was sure the old nun had won. Richard had to bluster and fulminate but it was not in his nature to deny such a request. Too often in the past, as he would never admit, such a gathering at Walton Street had proved a breakthrough. When he did agree, it was on his own terms.

"I will be bringing her by," he said, as if changing the subject. "I want her to see that upstairs bedroom and what's left of the computer."

"That's a splendid idea. Ten o'clock would be best for us."

Mr. Rush agreed to bring the Laytons and wild horses could not have kept Katherine away.

8

Benjamin Rush introduced the Laytons to Sister Mary Teresa who squeezed the grieving mother's hand while Geoffrey Layton tried not to stare at the old nun's habit. He looked around the room as if fearful of what signs of superstition he might find, but a man who could get used to the shrine in the hallway of his own house had little to fear on Walton Street. Katherine swept in, a glint in her eye. At the street door she'd whispered that she couldn't wait to see how Emtee Dempsey broke the shell of Miss Butterfingers.

Kim said nothing. It was unnervingly clear that Emtee Dempsey meant to exonerate the convicted terrorist. Katherine might soon be witnessing the first public embarrassment of her old friend rather than another triumph. Janet was in the kitchen talking with Joyce so Kim answered the door when Richard arrived. Regina Fastnekker stood beside him, hands joined in front of her, linked with cuffs, but her expression was serene. Behind them were Gleason and O'Connell, shifting their weight and looking up and down the street. Kim stepped aside and they trooped in.

"Okay if we just go upstairs?"

"The others are in the living room."

Richard ignored that and proceeded up the stairs with his prisoner. O'Connell leaned close to Kim. "Who's here?"

"I'll introduce you."

Gleason tugged O'Connell's arm and shook his head warningly. They would stay right where they were.

When Richard came into the living room, one hand on Regina's elbow, he feigned surprise at the people gathered there.

"I'm here for an on-site inspection of the bombing," he announced to the far wall.

Mrs. Layton was staring with horror at Regina Fastnekker, and her husband looked murderously at the expressionless terrorist. Regina had an announcement of her own.

"Your automobile was blown up by Michael Layton," she said to Sister Mary Teresa.

"Get her out of here!" Geoffrey Layton cried. "Better yet, we'll go."

"Wait," Emtee Dempsey said. "Let us hear what Regina has to say."

She repeated, "Michael Layton blew up your car. I called him as soon as I heard of it on the news." She moved closer to the old nun. "He despised me for being born again. He meant to force my hand."

Geoffrey Layton sneered. "He blew up their car and then blew up himself and then blew up the sisters' computer? Is that your story?"

"Did you kill Michael Layton?" Sister Mary Teresa asked Regina.

"No."

The old nun shifted her hands on the arms of her chair. "Did you do anything that resulted in the death of Michael Layton?"

Regina started. But she did not answer. She looked warily, almost fearfully at the old nun.

"I know you express yourself with great precision," Emtee Dempsey said. "One who has vowed always to tell the truth must be most precise in what he says. I ask you again. Did you do anything that . . ."

"Yes!"

A smile broke out on Richard's face and he looked as if he might actually hug Emtee Dempsey.

"But you didn't murder him?"

"No."

"Richard, let our guest sit down so that she can speak at her leisure."

But Regina shook her head. She preferred to speak standing. "Michael blew up your car, using skills we had learned together. This consisted in planting the device and from a distance activating it. After Michael's phone call, I drove past his house with a transceiver set at the appropriate frequency."

"And there was an explosion."

"Yes."

"So you killed him!" Richard said.

"No. He killed himself. That radio signal could only harm him if he intended to harm someone else. If a man fires at another and his gun backfires and kills him, has his intended victim killed him or has he killed himself?"

It was a discussion that went on for some time. The general consensus in the room was that Regina was lying, blaming a dead man.

"That's how she planned it," Geoffrey Layton said with disgust.

Benjamin Rush sat sunk into himself. Nothing Geoffrey Layton could say would restore his son's honor.

Emtee Dempsey rose and went to Mrs. Layton who was looking around almost wildly, as if she could not at all understand what was going on. Kim felt much the same way. Her eye met Janet's and she went to her. How awful this must be for her. But Janet did not want to be consoled.

"I'm leaving," she said, and started for the kitchen door.

"Wait, my dear." Surprisingly Emtee Dempsey was at Kim's side. She took Janet's hand authoritatively and led her to Regina.

"Regina Fastnekker," she said, "did you give this girl computer disks to pass on to me?"

Regina looked surprised for the second time.

"No."

"You are not dissembling, are you?"

Regina peered at Janet. "Is that how it was done?"

Janet lunged at Regina who lifted her manacled hands and staved off the blow. By then Emtee Dempsey had again grasped Janet's wrist and Richard had come to her assistance.

"We're talking about the device that blew up the computer?"

"She's the one," Janet screamed, trying to free herself. "She ruined Michael's life and he waited for her while she was in jail and out she comes a religious freak. No more terrorism for Miss Butterfingers."

Janet threw back her head and began to howl in frustration. Her father seemed to age before their eyes and Mrs. Layton recoiled from the spectacle of her out-of-control daughter. Benjamin Rush tried to calm Janet, but she lowered her shoulder and bumped him away, very nearly sending him to the floor. That's when O'Connell and Gleason came in and subdued her. It seemed a good idea to unshackle Regina and put the cuffs on Janet. Katherine Senski stood, looked around the room and asked if she could use the study. She had a story to write.

★ ★ ★ ★ ★

But her story was incomplete until two days later when a defiant but subdued Janet told of rigging the disks in order to turn suspicion firmly on Regina. The woman had ruined Michael's life and Janet was sure she had killed him as well. By continuing with her brother's plan she hoped to send Regina Fastnekker back to prison.

That, as it turned out, was her own destination, however postponed it would be, given the legal counsel her parents hired for her defense. She released a statement saying that she regretted that anything she might have done had threatened the nuns on Walton Street. But by then she had reverted to her story that Regina Fastnekker had persuaded her to deliver the disks.

Questioned about this at the mall where she was urging shoppers to repent and be saved, Regina would say only, "When I was a child I spoke as a child but now that I have become a man I have put away the things of a child."

Emtee Dempsey asked Katherine if her paper's policy would necessitate altering the scriptural passage cited by Miss Butterfingers, but her old friend pretended not to hear.

The Other Urn

A Sister Mary Teresa Mystery

1

When Bridget Barry, who had taught Renaissance History at the College once owned and operated by the Sisters of Martha and Mary (the M&M's), came to visit Sister Mary Teresa in the house on Walton Street in Chicago, it was time to kill the fatted calf. Which, Joyce suggested to Kim, might be Bridget herself. She had put on weight, no doubt of that, but then Emtee Dempsey was a bit of a butterball herself. They made a pair.

Sister Mary Teresa (Emtee) Dempsey still wore the traditional headdress of the order, which gave the general impression of a seagull landing on her head. A starched wimple, black robes, a rosary clacking from her cincture—she had been dressing like this for over fifty years and she did not intend to change now. Kim and Joyce, on the other hand, dressed like anyone else, except for a cross, pinned to their lapel, indicating their religious profession. The three of them in this house on Walton Street were all that was left of the M&M's. They had renewed almost into oblivion, selling off their college, a money-losing enterprise at the time, and turning to more relevant work. That had resulted in a mass exodus from the order.

"Who would have dreamed it would come to this?"

Bridget asked, but Emtee Dempsey waved away such keening with a pudgy hand.

"The three of us are carrying on. If God wants His order to go on, He will send us vocations."

"You can't complain about your accommodations," Bridget said. Kim had given her a tour of the house which was designed by Frank Lloyd Wright, and now sat with their guest in the study where Sister Mary Teresa each day added her quota of pages to the massive history of the 12th century she was writing.

"How long will you be doing research at the Newberry, Bridget?"

"Another week, more or less."

Brows rose above the old nun's round spectacles. "How long have you been in Chicago without contacting me?"

Bridget was having none of that. "In the first place, you are very hard to find. I phoned Katherine Senski and she gave me your number. Why an unlisted number?"

"You said in the first place."

"Yes." Bridget's merry face darkened. "Do you remember Vivian Green, one of our alumnae?"

The old nun shut her eyes. You could almost hear the whirring. "Class of '75. Black hair, ivory skin? She got a B – in medieval history."

"Well, she got an A+ in Renaissance History. You were always stingy with high grades."

"Because God is stingy with brains. What about Vivian?"

"We've kept in touch. She was admitted to the graduate school at the University of Chicago but in the first semester decided it was not for her. Now stop nodding as if some theory of yours had been proved. She had the talent; she didn't have the interest. She switched to law."

Emtee Dempsey groaned. "Another! What on earth will we do with all these lawyers?"

"Vivian passed the bar but she has never practiced law in the usual sense. She got a job as vice director and subsequently became director of a small foundation. She has done very well. Beautiful apartment, not far from here, a very posh lakeside address. She looks out over the lake."

"So you found time to visit her?" Emtee Dempsey began.

"Not this time. That's what worries me. At the foundation, my call wasn't put through, and then when I called her at home, she made it very brief. I had come at just the wrong time."

Kim said, "Maybe if you had let her know you were coming."

"I did. I dropped her a note over a month ago, asking that she reply only if this would not be a good time for us to get together." Bridget, who had been sitting forward, deflated visibly while saying this.

"It's not at all like Vivian."

Maybe yes, maybe no. Kim wondered if the younger woman had really been that enthralled to see her old professor. However brilliant she was, Bridget Barry was not a very prepossessing figure.

Before Bridget left, promises were made all around that they would get together for a really good session before Emtee Dempsey's former colleague left Chicago.

"What we will do," Sister Mary Teresa said when their guest was gone, "is have a tribute to Bridget Barry by a small group of colleagues and selected former students. Particularly one." The old nun picked up her fountain pen, unscrewed its cap, and said to Kim, "Your job will be to contact Vivian Green. Find a time good for her and we will organize around that."

"Maybe she just doesn't want to keep up the contacts."

"Nonsense. She was completely devoted to Bridget."

"Well, there could be other reasons."

"Precisely."

She pulled a piece of paper toward her and soon the room was filled with the sound of pen on paper. Kim had been dismissed. Dismissed with a task. It was infuriating how Emtee Dempsey put the weight of her whims on other shoulders. Kim turned on her heel and went into the kitchen. Something fragrant was in the oven. Joyce in slacks and a sweatshirt with the legend Universidad de Salamanca emblazoned on it sat at the table frowning over a crossword.

"We are going to have a little party for Bridget Barry."

"Good. What does magisterial mean?"

"You see it everyday, in the study."

"Fat?"

"Joyce! Speaking with a master's authority." Then she asked, "Do you remember a student named Vivian Green?"

"Sure." Joyce didn't even look up.

"Are you serious?"

"She played soccer." Joyce looked at Kim and added, "Not well, but with enthusiasm."

Kim went to the stove and poured herself a cup of coffee. Emtee Dempsey had remembered Vivian Green and now Joyce acted as if she had seen her just the other day. Kim said as much.

"I did. Well, not the other day. She lives around here. I saw her in that little gourmet store several blocks over when I was getting the caviar Emtee was sure Mr. Rush would like." Rush was their lawyer; he hadn't liked the caviar.

"It must be some other lawyer who likes it," the old nun had said, regaining the upper hand. Rush spent the rest of the evening trying not to ask if she were consulting someone else.

Not very likely. Rush had been on the board of the college and had maneuvered them through the difficult times that ended with their keeping this house on Walton Street as well as some lake property in Indiana.

"Did you talk to her?" Kim asked Joyce.

"A little. She looked very prosperous, though. I mentioned the soccer and I thought she was going to cry. You know how it is when you seem to remind someone of better days? I felt like that."

"I have the job of making sure she comes to the party for Bridget."

"The way she acted, anything connected with her college days would be attractive to her."

It was a temptation to shift the burden to Joyce's shoulders, but Kim did not succumb. Emtee Dempsey almost never put things in terms of obedience, but she was Kim's religious superior. And there was a definite division of labor in this diminished community. Joyce's province was the kitchen and household. Kim was in graduate school at Northwestern but also Emtee Dempsey's research assistant, a function the old nun interpreted in a very commodious manner. Kim would not have been human if she did not sometimes feel resentment, but she had not become a nun for the fun of it.

Emtee Dempsey had played a large role in Kim's vocation. The combination of great intellect and a religious life had a powerful appeal, and the appeal had survived the tumultuous days when they had closed the college, handed out the money they got for it, and begun to swim in the sea of the people. When things settled down, Kim retained her desire to lead her life as Emtee Dempsey had hers, although what that meant in the present state of affairs was unclear. But then she had learned to trust in God from the old nun too.

Green, Vivian was not in the telephone directory. Nor any

Green, V. She worked for a small foundation, Bridget had said, but Kim could not go by the Newberry and ask the name of it. This was supposed to be a surprise. She put through a call to Katherine Senski, the veteran writer for the *Tribune*, fellow campaigner with Emtee Dempsey whose junior she claimed improbably to be. Nonetheless, she had retained her job at the *Tribune* through recent changes in ownership and continued to do features. Like Emtee she would not know what retirement meant even if she were doing a crossword puzzle.

"Bridget Barry! Of course I'll come. It's a splendid idea. Actually I think we ought to do something far more grand. A reunion of all former faculty and students."

"Katherine, wait. We won't even have this small get together if I can't locate Vivian Green."

"Who's Vivian Green?"

"Thank God you don't know."

"You are being enigmatic, Sister Kimberly."

"She was a student of Bridget's, they have kept in touch. Bridget is now in town and Vivian is too busy to see her and Bridget is convinced something is wrong."

"Has it occurred to Bridget that her conversation might not be as scintillating to a young woman as you and I find it?"

"When did I cease being a young woman?"

"Take it as a compliment, for heaven's sake. I don't want you getting sensitive."

"The received opinion is that Vivian genuinely admires Bridget Barry, and would not miss a chance to see her if she could."

"She might be genuinely busy, my dear."

"That is what I have to find out."

"Well, call her."

Finally they had arrived at the point of the call. Katherine hummed while Kim explained, then said, "My dear, the listing of private foundations in this country demands two extremely stout volumes. The Illinois section, as I remember, runs pages and pages."

"It is a small family foundation."

"Most of them are. Most of them are fairly obvious dodges enabling the wealthy to distribute their own excess income rather than let the government do it. Often they have a single purpose, very narrowly defined."

Katherine was defining an impossible task. "Of course I am. This is another argument for keeping up the alumnae directory. Rush can complain about expense. I say charge a fee. Alumnae want to keep in touch and women have this medieval habit of changing their names when they marry."

"It is not a medieval habit. It was not done then."

"Is that true?" Katherine was delighted.

"I have it on the highest authority."

"How long has Vivian Green worked with this foundation?"

But Kim had had the thought herself. As one of the foes of another edition of the alumnae directory, she must have wiped it from her mind. The donkey work had of course devolved on Kim and a new edition would cost her at least another year before she completed her dissertation. "I'll look her up."

"I am doing that now. You say your job is research assistant? Ah, here it is. The Apeiron Foundation. Well, they didn't use the family name. Got a pencil."

Kim jotted down the address and it was indeed nearby. She took down the telephone number too but decided to go in person. She did not want to risk a repetition of the treatment Bridget Barry had received.

The Apeiron Foundation was in Evanston, and when Kim's taxi arrived at the address she was surprised to find that it was in a residential neighborhood and, like its neighbors, a private house. She felt vaguely like a saleslady standing on the doorstep after ringing the bell. Avon calling.

After a decent interval, she rang again. Almost immediately the door opened and a forbidding looking man of middle height looked impatiently out at her.

"I've come to see Vivian Green."

He stepped to one side to let her pass, still frowning. She waited until he had closed the door, then followed him. The smell of flowers was heavy in the house and it seemed ill lit. Her guide led the way to an open door, then again stood aside. Kim started into the room, then stopped with a gasp.

The burnished urn was enshrined on an altar with a photograph propped up behind it, surrounded by flowers. The light was muted, there was a prie-dieu. Kim moved toward the open casket, knelt and looked at the photographed features of what had once been a beautiful young woman.

2

Some minutes later, Kim rose from her knees and turned. The man in the doorway was not the one who had answered the door. White unruly hair, a stoop that seemed an apology for his height, penetrating blue eyes that searched Kim's face. He held out his hand.

"Ambrose Ellis." The words seemed to ride a musical undertone.

"Sister Kimberly Moriarity."

"Sister?" Thick white brows knit.

"Yes. I am a member of the Order whose college Vivian attended."

"Ah."

"This is quite a shock," Kim said with feeling.

He nodded as if between them they carried the weight of the world. Then he took her elbow and steered her to another room. An office.

"She worked here," Ellis said. "It seems only yesterday that I hired her."

"The Apeiron Foundation."

He nodded and then he scrutinized her again. "How did you learn of her death?"

Emtee Dempsey would have had a dozen ways of answering that question which, if not lies in the estimation of the old nun, would have been guaranteed to convey to Ambrose Ellis that she had come here knowing Vivian Green was dead. Kim lacked this talent, if that was the right name for it.

"I came here expecting to find her alive."

His mouth opened and closed in silent anguish. "Oh my. Are you Professor Barry?"

"No. But it is because of her I came. How long had Vivian been ill?"

"Ill? She wasn't ill at all. She was struck down by an automobile." A pause. "Why did you think she was ill?"

"Professor Barry said she sounded preoccupied. She had hoped to get together with Vivian, who was an old student, and was put off."

"And she sent you?" Clearly he found this strange. But Kim did not have to answer. A bell rang, very loudly, and hardly stopped before it began again. There was the quick sound of footsteps and the man who had let her in hurried by. The bell sounded a third time and then the door opened.

"It's about time," a male voice said impatiently. "Where is Ambrose?"

But he did not wait for an answer. Suddenly he was there

in the doorway, a man of perhaps thirty, open shirt, sport coat, bearded. His eyes darted from Ellis to Kim and back.

"Where is she?"

"James, you are understandably upset . . ."

"Upset! Is it true? I don't believe it. Where is she?"

Ambrose Ellis tried to take the younger man's arm but he shook it free.

"What have you done to her?"

"Come with me. I'll take you to her."

Kim felt like a thing. James ignored her; Ellis did not introduce her. She went to the door and watched as Ellis took the visitor to the room where Vivian lay. James let out a cry, of rage, of despair, and then went into the room. In a moment there was the rending sound of his sobbing. Ellis turned around to find Kim watching and his expression appealed for sympathy.

"I'm sorry. The poor poor fellow. I'll show you to the door, Sister."

"Who is he?"

"James Parnell. An artist. One of the recipients of an Apeiron Fellowship. Vivian was always supportive of his applications. Not that he was a successful artist, but she almost took that as an endorsement."

"When will the funeral be?"

"I thought we would have a ceremony at the gravesite."

"But won't there be a funeral Mass?"

He thought about it. "Perhaps she would have liked that."

"Isn't there any family?"

"Just myself."

"You're a relative?"

He looked at her almost suspiciously. "I am her husband." And then, as if trying the new formulation for the first time, "I was her husband. We married just a month ago."

3

The get-together was not the one Sister Mary Teresa had planned. When Kim returned, Katherine Senski was already at the house on Walton Street, wearing a purple dress that represented an extravagant waste of material with folds and overlaps, and skirts under skirts, as if Katherine were emerging from a fabric telescope.

"That girl was dead even as we talked about her," Katherine said.

She sat across the desk from Emtee Dempsey in the book-lined study and spoke as if Kim should somehow have known this.

"I have just seen the body."

"Always check the morgue. A cub reporter knows that and I forgot."

"She wasn't missing, Katherine," Emtee Dempsey said soothingly. "Why don't we let Sister Kimberly tell us what she has learned?"

The two old women listened attentively as Kim made her report and the old nun's first reaction was to call the cathedral parish and make arrangements for a funeral Mass. "When? It may have to be tomorrow morning. Take down this address."

She hung up. "Now then, what did you learn from James Parnell?"

"Nothing. I left while he was still weeping beside the casket."

"With the husband looking on," Katherine murmured.

"He said she was struck down by a car, Katherine?"

"Hit and run. Two days ago. She wasn't identified immediately."

"She hadn't been reported missing, had she?"

Katherine had the look of a student who can't think of answer. "May I use your telephone?"

"To call the police? I suggest that we have Sister call her brother Richard."

"I have contacts of my own," Katherine said with an edge to her voice.

"I know. But Richard is so helpful."

Kim said, "Maybe Katherine should call someone else."

"Nonsense. Richard would never forgive me."

That at least was true, though not in the sense the old nun intended. There was a friendly enmity between her and Kim's brother Richard, Detective Lieutenant in the Chicago police. He was always enraged by her intrusions into his work, yet more often than not happy enough to take advantage of the wisdom Emtee Dempsey had gathered in over seven decades, from personal experience, from the vicarious experience she had derived from her study of history, and from over thirty years in the classroom.

Kim made the call in the kitchen, after telling Joyce of her visit.

"The wake was in the house? I didn't know that was done anymore."

"There wasn't even going to be a funeral, Joyce."

Joyce made a face. "I can still see her playing soccer. If she lived the way she played, she must have been something."

Richard answered the phone, said just a minute and then left it open for five minutes while unintelligible babble came through to her.

"What is it, Kim?" he said when he returned.

"One of Sister Mary Teresa's former students was killed in a hit and run and she wondered if you knew anything about it."

"A hit and run," he said patiently. "Kim, I am in homicide."

"Her name was Vivian Green and . . ."

"What! Do you mean Vivian Ellis?"

"We didn't know she was married until a few hours ago."

"Kim, how in the hell did she get mixed up in this one?"

"That's what she wants to tell you."

"Well put her on."

"She would appreciate it a lot if you could come here, Richard."

She held the phone away from her ear, then covered it with her hand lest Joyce be contaminated by Richard's ire. After a moment, she spoke into it.

"When can we expect you?"

"Within the hour."

Kim went back to the study with what Emtee Dempsey at least would consider good news. Ten minutes later Bridget Barry arrived and Kim had to tell her story again and this was the most difficult time of all.

"Dead?" Bridget looked stunned. "But I talked to her only a few . . ."

"Sit down, Bridget. We will get to the bottom of this; you can depend upon that. Sister, have Sister Joyce put on tea. Katherine, will you have tea?"

"Not until after I have had a glass of sherry."

Emtee Dempsey nodded to Kim.

Bridget said, "If you have bourbon, bring me some of that."

It was not much more than a hour later when, transferred to the living room, the posthumous get-together for Vivian Green took place. Richard was a bit wary with Mr. Rush, Kim thought, and vice versa. Perhaps there is some natural antagonism between lawmen and lawyers, though Mr. Rush had never defended a criminal. ("Other than myself," Emtee Dempsey would remind her.) Three elderly women, an elderly lawyer and two Moriaritys, herself and Richard. Richard was drinking beer.

"The Apeiron Foundation," Mr. Rush repeated, putting down his scotch. It was in deference to his legendarily moderate drinking habits that Emtee Dempsey kept a good supply of beverages for the entertainment of guests. Rush took out a leather enclosed notebook and wrote it down. "Foundations report regularly to the Secretary of State. I will have a check made on the . . ." He squinted at his note. "The Apeiron Foundation."

"The word means boundless," Emtee Dempsey said. "By extension, eternal."

Mr. Rush's mouth twisted in a little smile. "A modest ambition when setting up a foundation."

Bridget Barry said, "The idea was to promote artists whose works would last. Vivian explained it to me."

"The family must contain a classical scholar," Katherine said. She was seated next to Mr. Rush as usual, but the handsome widower seemed impervious to her charms.

"Or their lawyer is more learned than most."

"Ellis the husband mentioned her devotion to Professor Barry here," Richard said. "In fact, he says the accident occurred just as she was on her way to visit her."

"Had she bought a ticket?" Emtee Dempsey asked.

"She was going to buy it at Midway."

"Was the trip on the spur of the moment?"

Richard turned to Bridget Barry. "Had she told you she was coming to see you?"

"No. But I had urged her to. She worked too hard. She hadn't had a real vacation in three years."

Katherine said, "Wouldn't there have been a honeymoon?" She reached across Mr. Rush for an ashtray but he swiftly handed it to her. She smiled at him as if the gesture were worth a million words.

"Look," Richard said. "I understand your curiosity. She went to the college. She remained a friend. Fine. But what we have here is a hit and run. It is not in my jurisdiction. It is being investigated, but there has been no questioning of the family. Why should there be?"

"Richard is perfectly correct," Emtee Dempsey said, as if stilling an uprising. "Until it is clear her death was homicide, he and his colleagues will not conduct the necessary interviews. That leaves it up to us."

"No, it doesn't! Sister Mary Teresa, please. For once leave well enough alone. You have a book to write. You have prayers to say."

"Yes, and I must no doubt meet my maker soon. I do not wish to appear before Him with great sins of omission on my conscience. I do not for a minute believe Vivian Green died as the victim of an automobile accident. I hope the clothes she was wearing were sent to the lab."

Richard nodded, a picture of a man barely keeping control of himself. Kim sympathized with him; as his sister she knew how annoying to him Sister Mary Teresa's interventions must be. The trouble was there always seemed to be an excuse. Vivian had been a student of the college, she was remembered by the old nun and she was the friend of an esteemed former colleague, Bridget Barry. There was no way in the world Emtee Dempsey would rest until she knew exactly what happened. But what she could not know, Kim was sure, was that Vivian Green's death was not accidental. Richard made the same point.

"What flight had she planned to take?"

Richard checked a piece of paper. "An 11:45 a.m. to Tampa St. Petersburg."

"Exactly."

"Exactly what?"

"You said her body was found on Chase Avenue. It would be difficult to be farther from Midway and still be in Chicago. What was she doing there? When did her husband say she left the house?"

"She had less than an hour before the flight."

"And within that hour she thought she had time to detour to Chase Street, dismiss her cab—you will have to check on the cab, of course—and manage to be struck by an automobile. No, it was not an accident."

"Sister Mary Teresa," Richard said patiently. "Until and unless this is declared a homicide, it will be investigated as a hit and run. Which means we are looking for the driver of the car. We don't care what she was doing on Chase Street. For all we know, she changed her mind and decided not to go to Florida. Maybe that was an excuse to get out of the house."

"Good! These are the avenues that have to be explored."

Richard rose, bowed exaggeratedly to Emtee Dempsey and then directed a sweet smile around the group until he got to Kim and it faded. "Don't think it hasn't been nice."

"You've been immensely helpful, Richard, and we are grateful."

"I wish I hadn't come," he said with feeling.

4

Chase Street was in the neighborhood of Old Town but with none of the restored éclat of that area. The block on which Vivian had been struck was lined with cars on both sides, bumper to bumper almost, leaving only a narrow passageway for traffic. It seemed to Kim that a pedestrian in that narrow street would have nowhere easily to go if a car came along at great speed. To squeeze between the parked cars to the sidewalk would be difficult. She wondered how the owner of one of these parked cars managed to drive it away, so wedged in were they.

The street was one of store fronts, Chinese restaurants, a pizzeria, bars. The buildings were four or five stories high and only their upper floors were residential.

Kim could easily imagine someone in a hurry, someone with a plane to catch, dashing into the street and being trapped as a car rushed down on her. An accident? Why not? But what had brought her to this part of Chicago when she had so little time if she were to catch the plane to Florida?

She was standing between a bar and an arts good store and someone hurried past, then stopped and turned. James Parnell.

"What are you doing here?" he asked.

"This is where it happened."

His bellicose manner dissolved and Kim feared he was going to break down again. He nodded, his mouth a thin line.

"Did you come to see it too?" she asked.

He began to nod then changed his mind and shook his head. "I live here."

"I see."

"I have a studio. Come on, I'll show it to you. What was your name again?"

"Kim. Sister Kimberly."

He glanced at her as they walked along. "What are you, Salvation Army or what?"

"I'm a nun."

"You're kidding. Vivvy went to school with the nuns."

"I know. She attended our college."

They had come to an entrance that led deep into a narrow, dark and smelly hallway. "Hope your legs are good. I'm at the top."

The stairs were no better than the hall but when they

reached the top they came into a huge undivided room lit by an enormous skylight. It was the very picture of the artist's studio.

"What a magnificent place."

"Do you drink coffee?"

"Please."

There was a bed at one end of the room and a makeshift kitchen but the rest was devoted to the studio's reason for being. There was a canvas on an easel that had been covered with a primer. Stacked against the walls were paintings.

How to describe them? There was something of Goya in them, a combination of realism and fancy, a figure floating above a room where two others spoke. But her eye was caught by a very large, very straightforward portrait.

"Isn't that Vivian?"

"In the flesh."

No exaggeration there, God knew. But there was a kind of modest defiance in her nudity that gave Kim a sense of the woman in the way the photo in the shrine at the Apeiron Foundation had not.

"She modeled for you?"

He handed her a cup of coffee and looked her in the eye. "We were in love."

"What happened?"

"Nothing happened!"

Kim sipped her coffee. She had to press the matter or Emtee Dempsey would never forgive her. "But she married Ambrose Ellis."

"Yes, she did," he said furiously. He drew back his hand as if he meant to dash his coffee on the canvas with Vivian's picture. Kim put a hand on his arm.

"Don't."

He looked at her. "I couldn't." He inspected the picture.

"It is a very good likeness. Portraiture is not my gift. Look at this one of Pilar. But I was inspired this once. And there is much more than her surface here." A look of anguish came over him. "I wanted her to quit work, come here, live with me."

Before or after her marriage to Ambrose? But James had turned to her again.

"I killed her."

He said it calmly and, Kim thought, with a certain relief. Suddenly the studio no longer seemed as capacious as it had. She thought of the long dark hallway and all those stairs they had climbed. Now here she was alone with a very upset man who said he had killed Vivian.

"You were driving the car?"

"No. I don't even have a car. She was convinced that one day I would be famous and rich. Maybe after I'm dead. Right now I don't own a bicycle."

"She was killed by a car."

"Yes. And right below in that street. Why was she there?"

"She had come to see you?"

He laughed a bitter laugh. "Sure. Because I had made the ultimate appeal. I told her I was going to kill myself. That is why she came. That is why she was in the street when some maniac came along and killed her." He gave her a haunted look. "And I didn't know she had come. I thought she recognized my bluff and went off to Florida as she planned. And she was lying down there dead, under a car, undiscovered."

5

The services for Vivian Green were held in the little chapel in the house on Walton Street. A father in California could not come. He was institutionalized and past feeling any grief at the loss of his daughter, if he even remembered he had one. It was the saddest funeral Kim had ever seen, yet it could have been worse. It might not have happened at all. Ambrose Ellis sat uncomfortably in a front pew with a much made-up middle-aged woman he had identified as his sister. The little man who had answered the door at the Apeiron Foundation stood in the back. Obviously none of them was Catholic. Bridget Barry and Katherine and Florence Dodge, president of Vivian's class, sat together, while Emtee Dempsey, Joyce and Kim knelt together. Father Foy said the Mass of the Angels, a liturgy full of the joy of resurrection, but Kim felt a powerful urge to weep. She wondered if Ambrose Ellis had told the artist James Parnell of the service. His grief when he went into that little shrine containing her ashes had been genuine.

The urn stood on a table in the aisle of the chapel. From time to time, Ambrose Ellis would turn to look at it, almost in disbelief. Vivian had been his wife for a month and now she was dead.

After the memorial service, Ambrose Ellis began by saying how grateful he was to Kim and her colleagues for the wonderful service. "Both Pilar and I were deeply moved. My sister and I are not of your faith, but Vivian would have wanted such a service."

Kim said, "I went to Chase Street where it happened and ran into James Parnell."

"Poor James. Did you talk? He was in love with Vivian, you know. At least he thought it was. He had convinced himself they were meant to play out some grand and tragic passion together. It was quite embarrassing to Vivian and not a little annoying to me."

"It continued after you married Vivian?"

"James as an artist cannot recognize marriage as an impediment to his appetites." He smiled. "One thing is certain, however. He has undeniable talent. Even genius. For that we forgave him much."

"Why would Vivian have been there when she had to catch a plane?"

"I am guessing of course, but he must have threatened suicide again."

"Again?"

"Life without her was meaningless, he had no reason to go on." Ambrose's voice became theatrical. But then a profoundly sad expression came over his face.

"But it was her he killed, wasn't it? Now he must live with that. As for me, I am grateful for the little month we had."

Kim was assailed by thoughts of the canvas of the nude Vivian in James's studio. And she had been on her way to Florida, a separate vacation after a month of marriage. But it would take an Emtee Dempsey to probe beneath the surface of Ambrose Ellis. But the old nun led Bridget Barry down the hall to her study, comforting her grieving former colleague.

6

Mr. Rush did not wish to comment one way or another on the facts about the Apeiron Foundation he had discovered.

"Perhaps they speak for themselves. What is simply factual is that the initial endowment of some eighty million has dwindled over the past three years to less than twenty. This means that capital was being disbursed and not merely interest on capital, in itself an extraordinary procedure for a foundation of this kind. Not illegal, precisely, but perhaps not within the constituting documents of the Apeiron Foundation either."

"Who did set it up?" Emtee Dempsey asked. She and the lawyer and Kim were in the old nun's study. Rush had telephoned to say he would like to drop by to pass on what he had learned of the foundation for which Vivian had worked.

"Mr. Ellis. The father of Ambrose and Pilar. With a quite well defined purpose of supporting the arts. The brother and sister, together with some aged relatives, constitute the board."

"To whom has the money gone?"

Mr. Rush nodded in approval of the question. "An entity called Video Beat whose professed purpose is to elevate the musical taste of the nation's youth by producing video cassettes which will merge the modern and the classical."

"Video Beat. Who runs it?"

"Here is where things get slightly incestuous. Ambrose Ellis is president, but a flamboyant fellow named Sancho O'Neil is the actual manager. It is a non-profit company. In every sense of the term. To say it has been a flop would be kind. It has been devouring Apeiron money and Ambrose's reaction, egged on by Sancho O'Neil, is to pour in more money. A classical case. The gambler who thinks one more bet will right the scales, the investor who thinks if he can float one more loan he will recoup his losses. Clearly, to continue along this route will shortly drain the foundation of funds."

"And Ambrose has the right to do that if he wishes?"

"If he has the backing of his board."

"And he does?"

Mr. Rush had the look of a man about to play the forgotten trump. "A week ago an action was filed by Pilar Ellis and Mrs. Ambrose Ellis, on behalf of the foundation, asking the court to restrain Ambrose from dispensing any more funds and demanding his resignation as director."

"Mr. Rush, I congratulate you. This is important information indeed. What is the present status of the suit?"

"A restraining order has been issued. Ambrose's hands have been legally tied for some days now."

"How many days?"

"Four."

"The day Vivian left for Florida. Is the foundation simply immobilized?"

"Pilar Ellis, in consultation with the court, will administer the foundation in the interim."

Sister Mary Teresa brought the fingers of her pudgy little hands together in an attitude of prayer. She must have been reviewing what Kim had told her of her earlier conversation with Ambrose because the old nun said, "I think I should like to have a talk with Ambrose Ellis."

"Not while I am present," Mr. Rush said, getting to his feet. Such was his admiration for the old nun that he seemed to think that all she had to do was express a wish to have it fulfilled. Kim knew otherwise.

"Sister Kimberly?"

"What could I possibly tell him that would induce him to come?"

"Tell him how much I regret that we saw one another on so sad an occasion when I had no chance to talk with him. I would like to repair the omission."

That at least had the semblance of truth about it. Once in answer to the question whether she had read all the books in her library, Emtee Dempsey had boldly replied, "I have read every word in every one of them."

Kim objected, later, if only because new books had been added that very week. Not that she believed the old nun had accomplished what she claimed with the others. Of course she had an explanation. "Sister Kimberly, when I do read those new books I doubt that I shall encounter a word I have not already read." Devious of course. But Kim did not doubt

Sister Mary Teresa's current desire to have a talk with Ambrose Ellis.

But after Mr. Rush left and before she could set out unwillingly to the address of the Apeiron Foundation, a call came from Richard.

"Kim, I am going to say this only once, but I mean it. I am holding you responsible if Emtee Dempsey interferes in this case. Understand? You are responsible!"

"Richard, in the first place, that is ridiculous. She is my superior, not the reverse. Second, what case are you talking about?"

He sighed into the phone. "The death of Vivian Ellis."

"Have you been transferred to hit and run?"

"It has been ruled a homicide."

"Why?"

"We located the car that hit her."

"Who does it belong to?"

"Numero Dos, the rental agency. It was rented by someone connected with the Apeiron Foundation and on the face of it things look odd. But we don't want to make a lot of noise and above all I don't want you-know-who stirring up things."

"Who rented the car?"

"An artist who had been supported by the foundation. James Parnell."

"But that's impossible!"

"Do you know him?"

"I talked with him. Richard, he loved her. He wouldn't have done anything to harm her."

"Maybe you can testify for him in court."

"Richard, there has to be a mistake."

"The only mistake you have to worry about is your getting mixed up in this any further."

The phone went dead. Kim hung up, looked toward the study and then toward the kitchen. But she decided on the chapel where she could sit in silence and ask what was going on. This is where Vivian's ashes had been blessed and her soul commended to God's mercy. What had surrounded her death? She had been married a month, she was loved by James Parnell and had posed for him; she was engaged in a legal action against her husband in conjunction with his sister. And now the police thought James had driven the car that killed her. In circumstances as strange to her as these, who was Kim to say he could not have done it. She would not have given Richard the satisfaction of telling him that she knew instinctively that James was innocent. But it was true.

It was the thought of Pilar Ellis that seemed to be the light she sought. She would go to the sister first and then see what she could do about fulfilling the commission Emtee Dempsey had given her. Who but the old nun would regard it as routine that she summon a man like Ambrose Ellis to appear before her? Knowing what they now knew about him, they had to realize he might be less than eager to discuss either business or personal matters with virtual strangers.

Pilar said that of course she remembered Kim and would be happy to see her. Come right away if she could.

The address was on the north shore and there seemed to be a platoon of uniformed attendants to open the door, to call upstairs, to operate the elevator taking her to the uppermost floor from which Pilar Ellis looked both out onto the lake and southward to the loop.

"I love Chicago," she said, spreading her arms as if to embrace it. She wore a multi-colored caftan that made her seem a priestess asking a benediction on the city.

"James Parnell has been arrested," Kim said. "He is accused of driving the car that killed Vivian." It seemed important not to let Pilar write the script for this meeting.

"James! What nonsense." Pilar had turned in a swirl of caftan. "I will tell you a secret."

"He loved Vivian."

Pilar crossed the room and looked levelly at Kim, apparently deciding she was not a religious fanatic to be treated aloofly. "Please sit down. I am going to smoke. I presume you do not?"

Kim shook her head.

Having enveloped herself in clouds of cigarette smoke, Pilar said, "At the lovely ceremony you arranged at your house on Walton Street, I could not help but think how naive those are who act on a pious impulse. You assumed you were comforting a grieving husband. You have learned that James loved Vivian. Don't ask me why. These things never do make sense. There is good reason to think Vivian was fleeing to him on the pretense of going to Florida. It is a matter of great convenience for Ambrose that Vivian is dead."

"Because of the restraining order?"

Again Pilar looked at Kim more closely. "How do you happen to know of that? Not that it is a private matter."

"It came up when we were looking into the circumstances surrounding Vivian's death."

"Looking into? Do you mean investigating?"

"Sister Mary Teresa wants to know how and why Vivian died."

"How? She was struck by a car. Why?" Pilar smiled as smoke rolled from her mouth. "I found her an extremely difficult young woman to understand. Why, for example, did she marry Ambrose?"

"I wanted to ask you that."

"I don't know. Maybe every marriage resides on similar irrationality."

"Was it sudden?"

"I could not have been more surprised if she had married the mayor."

"Yet subsequently she joined with you in a law suit against her husband?"

"In the interests of the foundation."

"Where has all the money gone?"

"How much do you know?"

Kim gave a condensed version of what Mr. Rush had told Emtee Dempsey. For the third time Pilar was visibly impressed.

"Again, all that is in the public domain, but it is remarkable that you should have thought to look for it."

"Did Video Beat consume over fifty million in capital in three years?"

"Make it sixty. It did indeed, and was likely to need sixty more if it proved fair weather. The so-called entertainment industry has an insatiable maw. Millions mean nothing. We have always been wealthy, Ambrose and I, but the foundation is a small one as foundations go. He was well over his head the first month of his great adventure and he could not find the wisdom or the courage to admit he had made a mistake. Aided and abetted by one Sancho O'Neil, I might add."

"Where exactly did the money go?"

"Producers, musicians, distributors, duplicators, on and on. Oh, the bookkeeping was beyond reproach. Every ill-spent dollar is exquisitely accounted for. I tried logic, I tried pleading, finally I tried the law. So far that has been working. Ambrose will never forgive me. He insists he is on the verge of recouping all that has been invested and more, much more, besides. He apparently has learned nothing. He still thinks he has found a veritable gold mine."

"Aren't the films any good?"

"They are marvelous. They are not unpleasant to watch.

Alas, they do not appeal to the one group on which success depends. Sub teenagers. Imagine that. Ambrose put himself in thrall to children."

"Sister Mary Teresa wants to talk to Ambrose."

"A modest ambition."

"She never accepted Vivian's death as accidental. Now the police do not. Do you have any idea who might have killed her?"

Pilar leaned forward, shook her arm free in the massive sleeve, and crushed out her cigarette. "I can only eliminate people. It surely was not James. It just as surely was not Ambrose."

"Why not? Wasn't he angry with her for joining with you in the lawsuit?"

"He was furious, in his way. But he was so delighted with himself at having married Vivian he would certainly not have turned around and killed her. Besides, driving a car requires a physical coordination of which Ambrose is incapable. Nor did I kill her, incidentally. We had become allies, for one thing. For another, I would be incapable of such a deed."

"Sancho O'Neil."

She laughed. "Have you met him?"

"No."

"When you have, remember my reaction to your question."

"Is there anyone else?"

"Ames, who answers the door. Of course, there is always the possibility that what looks to have happened happened. Some careless fool ran into her and then drove away in panic. Imagine him, or her, waiting for a news story on what they had done."

"I visited James's studio."

"Did you really? I think he has real talent. He owes our

support of him to Vivian as much as anyone. She recognized what he had before Ambrose and I did. That is one of his paintings."

Kim had noticed it, a huge canvas opposite the windows opening to the east, yellows but carmine and umber as well, a scene emerging through a pastel fog, as of an advancing crowd about to break into the clear. There was menace in the picture.

"Does it have a name?"

" 'The Underground Men.' "

Approaching the painting, Kim noticed a pot almost concealed by the pulled drape. It reminded her of the urn she had seen at the Apeiron Foundation.

"I gave him thirty thousand dollars for it. His largest fee to date."

Then why did he continue to live where he did? But Kim, remembering that spacious studio, thought she understood. What does success do to artists, if not enable them to afford the things that dull their talent? But James had described himself as poor, unable to afford even a bike.

Apparently he had rented a car and run down the woman he loved. Kim did not want to believe that. She could not believe it. But how could she show it was false?

7

"By producing the one who did it," Emtee Dempsey answered. "It is always the only way. I do not say I share your conviction he is innocent, but neither am I convinced he is guilty."

"And who do you think might have done it?"

"Might have done it? Sister Kimberly, you or I might have done it. That is too large a category." She paused. "If only I had the chance to talk with Ambrose Ellis."

"He has agreed to come here tonight."

"I know you would not jest in so important a matter."

Pilar had called her brother before Kim left the apartment.

"Ambrose, Sister Kimberly, the pretty young woman with the red hair at Walton Street yesterday, is with me. She had the notion I might intercede for her with you. I explained our situation but am taking this chance anyway. I think we owe them something for the trouble they went to."

Her expression did not match the easy confidence of her words. When she had finished speaking, she winced and closed her eyes, listening. Her eyes opened and she gave Kim a look of exaggerated surprise and handed her the phone.

"Mr. Ellis?"

"You have a favor to ask?"

"Not for myself. Sister Mary Teresa, our superior, would so much like to speak with you and thought it inappropriate in the circumstances in which you first met. Could you come see her on Walton Street?"

"It would be a consolation, my dear, to talk with others who knew Vivian, particularly those who knew her when I did not."

"If you could come tonight . . ."

"Not for dinner, I'm afraid. Afterward?"

"Eight o'clock?"

"Eight thirty."

That easily it was done. But Kim did not regret having gone to Pilar first. In the meantime, she would go downtown and visit James Parnell.

Identifying herself as Richard's sister did wonders, although she felt guilty doing it, but soon she was looking at James Parnell through a cloudy glass, a phone to her ear.

"They think I did it." His voice was that of someone still stunned.

"They say you rented a car."

"Someone using a credit card of mine did."

"Was it stolen?"

"I didn't give it to anyone. I've been thinking and I'm sure I didn't. Anyone can just walk in my studio; you saw that. I figured those five flights of stairs are the best security I'll ever have."

"Did you tell the police that?"

"Sure. It got a big laugh." He leaned toward her. "This is like seeing someone through stained glass. I'd like to paint you."

"I saw the picture Pilar bought."

"The portrait I did of her?"

"No. 'The Underground Men.' "

He shrugged deprecatingly. "My yellow period. When I should have killed myself and didn't."

"Don't say that."

"It was bad when Vivian married Ambrose. I never had a good conversation with her after that. But at least she was somewhere, even if she wasn't with me. Now she's nowhere."

"That's not true."

He leaned forward again. "You believe all that?"

"I believe all that."

"I wish I did."

"Say your prayers." Kim smiled. "That is Pascal's advice, not mine."

"It sounds like my mother."

"Is she alive?"

"She just left. With my father. I'm not sure they believed me, so what can I expect of the police?"

"James, who killed her? You didn't. Someone did. Who?"

"My God, I don't know."

"It's the only way to get you out of here."

He didn't know and he wasn't good at imagining anyone killing Vivian. Ambrose? Why? Same with Pilar. Who else was there?

"James, do you know Sancho O'Neil?"

"Sancho." An almost tender smile came over James's face. "What a guy. He's spaced out on cloud nine half the time. Knows more about music than anyone I know, all kinds of music. Went to Eastman, went to Julliard. A genius. His problem is he can't take himself seriously. Vivian cut him off but he landed on his feet with Video Beat."

"Do you know how much money that effort has lost?"

"Lots. Sancho was playing with millions. He loved it. I saw several of his videos, MTV sorts of thing. Listen, in any genre genius can shine. They were marvelous."

"But they were losing money. Millions."

"Yeah." Again that tender smile as if commercial failure was a guarantee of the worth of what Sancho had done.

"But the point of Video Beat was to attract the young."

"The young?" James shook his head. "An artist doesn't aim. He makes and usually has to wait."

"Like you?"

"I'm young."

"James, didn't Pilar give you a large sum of money for that painting?"

He nodded. "I loaned it to Sancho. He had a cash problem."

"A cash problem! But he got millions from the Apeiron Foundation."

"Kim, I've got to get out of here."

"That's what we're talking about. Give me a suspect?"

He looked at her through that murky window for a full

minute, then shook his head. "I can't. To get out of here I'd blame my mother, but I know she didn't do it. What's the point of kidding myself? A stolen credit card. I may be laughing over that for years."

Kim reported this to Sister Mary Teresa and realized how tired she was. She had spent the day running around, to no purpose. And Ambrose would be coming after supper.

"Go take a nap, Sister. You deserve it."

"For wasting the day? Sister, you should see him there in jail. It's like caging a bird. How can I just go up and take a nap?"

"Because I will be putting my mind to it in the meantime. You may have found out more than you realize."

"What?"

A little pudgy finger waggled. "Go take your nap."

It was a soothing thought that she had unwittingly told Emtee Dempsey something the old nun could use as a key to decode this confusing set of events. Kim only wished that she believed it.

Kim answered the door that night at 8:40 to find Ambrose Ellis and another younger man on the doorstep.

"I have brought along a colleague, Sister. I hope that's all right."

"Of course. Sister Mary Teresa asked some others too."

"Oh? This is Sancho O'Neil." He added, after a pause, "The musician."

O'Neil was of middle height, boneless, a huge smile and eyes that were enlarged comically by extremely thick glasses. His clothes appeared to be draped on him and he moved to some inaudible music, though there were no headphones visible.

"Had to come, had to come. A convent? Man. Take five."

He showed her his palm and Kim obligingly laid her hand on his. He paid no attention, looking around once they were inside. Kim led them down the hall, hoping Joyce had been listening from the kitchen. Sister Mary Teresa would get quite a kick out of Sancho O'Neil. And vice versa.

Awaiting them in the living room, besides Richard and Mr. Rush, were Pilar, Katherine and their hostess.

"Ah," Emtee Dempsey said, quieting the room and extending her hand to Ambrose. "Our guest of honor." Her gaze turned to the mobile man beside him. "And this would be Sancho O'Neil."

"The same, milady. The very same." He took the old nun's hand and would have brought it to his lips if she had not prevented it. Instead she levered herself to her feet with the musician's assistance and introduced Ambrose to others in the room. Kim noticed Richard's interest in Sancho O'Neil, and when she had asked what the two new arrivals would have and went to the kitchen, Richard came with her.

"Did she invite that hophead O'Neil?"

"You know him?"

"Every narc in Illinois knows him. Wherever he is, dangerous substances are found, but the most he has ever been up for is possession of marijuana. Let me make a call. I'll go in the study."

"Sancho O'Neil," Joyce said, excited. "Have you heard his music?"

"Joyce, I never heard his name before."

"He is a biggie, I'll tell you that. Everyone expects him to do great things."

Sancho O'Neil seemed to be many things indeed. Kim took him the tomato juice he had asked for and gave Ambrose a scotch on the rocks.

Ambrose looked at Kim reproachfully. "You led me to understand she wanted a tête-à-tête with me. This is a party!"

"Things got out of hand."

"How long do you intend to keep James Parnell locked up?" Pilar demanded of Richard Moriarity. "He is no more guilty of killing Vivian than I am."

"He rented the car that killed her."

"Some clerk identified him?"

"It was his credit card and it was his signature."

"A forgery," Pilar said contemptuously.

"Who would do such a thing?" Emtee Dempsey asked.

Pilar seemed about to say but decided against it. With a bejeweled hand, she held her full skirt and crossed her legs, bringing her glass to her mouth at the same time. She might have been acting on a dare—but not Emtee Dempsey's.

"The name she would like to give is mine," Ambrose Ellis said in his sepulchral voice. "She thinks I have been a bad steward of the foundation."

"The court seems to agree with her," Mr. Rush said.

Ambrose nodded. "That is true. But I shall confound my enemies. And my sister."

"With Video Beat?" Katherine asked.

"With Video Beat. I only regret that Vivian did not live to see my vindication."

"Where is she interred?" Sister Mary Teresa asked.

"Sister, I must thank you for the wonderfully consoling memorial service you arranged here. It is exactly what Vivian would have wanted."

"She is enshrined, not interred," Pilar said.

"What was the name of the clergyman who conducted the service?" Ambrose asked.

But Emtee Dempsey ignored him. "What do you mean, enshrined?" she asked Pilar.

Ambrose said, "Sister Kimberly can describe the room to

you. At the foundation. I cannot bear separation from her. Not yet."

"Mr. O'Neil," the old nun said, dismissing the subject, "tell us about your musical project. Video Beat."

And in half intelligible half sentences, accompanied by a hundred reiterations of "You know" and "Man," the spacy musician described his plan to merge the current interests of kids with the musical classics.

It was a virtuoso performance and during it, Emtee Dempsey beckoned Richard to her, they whispered for a minute and then Richard withdrew. And Sancho O'Neil spoke on.

"It is an absurdity," Pilar said, when the musician paused for breath.

"Everyone who has watched the videos agrees they are excellently done," Ambrose said.

"And the Edsel was a well-made car. I only hope the foundation can recover from your act of faith."

"You don't object to discussing your differences?" Emtee Dempsey asked Ambrose and Pilar.

"My dear lady," Ambrose said, "they have been bruited about a courtroom for weeks. We have no secrets. I have been accused of incompetence and theft and everything else. 'How sharper than a serpent's tooth . . .' "

He rolled his eyes to the ceiling and held out his empty glass. Kim collected it and others and took them to the kitchen for refills.

"Richard left," Joyce said.

"I noticed."

"He said he would be back."

And so he was, an hour later. He did not sit down and, when the old nun turned to him, he became the focus of attention.

141

"Well, Richard Moriarity?"

"Ellis, you're under arrest. Would you like your rights explained?"

"Under arrest!" He looked around. "Is this a convent parlor game?"

"We've taken possession of the urn, Ellis. Let's go."

"Richard," Emtee Dempsey said. "Be fair and tell us what you have found."

"You took Vivian's urn!" Ambrose fell back in his chair as if wounded.

"With a court order," Richard said.

"Is nothing sacred?"

"You can't keep human remains like that, Ellis. It's against the law."

"But I was told . . ."

"Did you open the urn?" Emtee Dempsey asked.

"Just to verify the contents."

"And they were ashes?" the old nun asked.

Kim realized that everyone hung on Richard's answer. Ambrose looked at Richard with apprehensive dread, Sancho emerged from a cloud of smoke, leaning forward, and Mr. Rush and Katherine were motionless in expectation.

Pilar broke the silence. "What did you find, Lieutenant?"

"Ashes."

Sancho became agitated and moved toward Ambrose.

"What's going on, man?"

"Of course you found ashes," Ambrose said. "That is what the urn is for." His eyes drifted toward Pilar who met his questioning glance with defiance.

"I don't like this," Sancho said.

"Do be quiet," Ambrose suggested to his protégé.

"What don't you like, Mr. O'Neil?" Emtee Dempsey asked. "Are you surprised that the urn contains ashes?"

"Why should he be!" Ellis demanded, but there was an odd anguish in his voice.

"And what of you, Pilar?" the old nun asked. "Are you surprised?"

"That Ambrose wished to keep Vivian's ashes near him? Not at all. They were very devoted."

"And what will be found in the urn in your apartment, Pilar?"

"What are you talking about?"

"Sister Kimberly," Emtee Dempsey said.

"The urn behind the drape in your living room. It is identical to the one I saw at the Apeiron Foundation."

"Because you bought it from the same funeral home," the old nun said. "McDivitt's."

"Another urn?" Ambrose cried. "Lieutenant Moriarty, I suggest you get a court order and confiscate that one."

"I did."

"You did!"

Emtee Dempsey said, "Perhaps you would like to tell us what that one contained, Ambrose?"

There was something pathetic in Pilar's attempt to dash from the room. Richard moved and stood athwart her path and she came to a stop, wheeled and looked at Kim with hatred. "This is your doing!" And she swooped toward Kim, hands outstretched, her long nails descending. But Richard caught her arm and held her. She screamed in rage, but the voice of the old nun was quite audible.

"Don't leave now, Mr. O'Neil."

Sancho O'Neil was almost to the door and now broke into a run. But Gleason and O'Connell had been stationed by the front door and soon brought him back, writhing and cursing.

"What have you done to us, Pilar?" Ambrose asked sorrowfully.

143

"Done?" Sancho cried. "She double-crossed us, man, that's what."

"What is in the other urn, Richard?" Katherine asked.

He had gotten handcuffs on Pilar with a struggle. "Cocaine. A very valuable amount of cocaine."

Ambrose sighed and brought the back of his hand to his forehead. "I was trying to recoup the money Sancho had lost. Just this once . . ." And he began unconvincingly to weep.

"Pilar," Emtee Dempsey said. "You killed Vivian, didn't you?"

The handsome woman looked at the old nun with venom and then at Kim. She might have been a beautiful captured beast, something feline.

"Yes! Yes, I did!"

"You fool," Ambrose said. "You fool."

"You have all been very foolish," the old nun said. "But Pilar has been more than foolish."

8

Mr. Rush left after Richard and his companions had taken away the three culprits. But Katherine wanted a postmortem and Emtee Dempsey was happy enough to accommodate her. Kim's seeing the urn in Pilar's apartment was crucial, of course, but another item had been equally decisive.

"The other portrait in James Parnell's studio. It was of Pilar. The thought occurred to me that she was as enamored of the artist as he was of Vivian."

"Which would make her jealous?"

"Of course. She thought she had overcome the rivalry when Vivian married her brother. But it was clear that James Parnell still loved Vivian. By using his credit card when she rented the car, Pilar was avenging herself on Parnell too."

Bridget Barry shook her head. "I can't believe she married that man. She had come to despise him."

"I think we will find that pressure was put upon her."

"What kind of pressure?"

"How did she put it in her letter to you, Bridget? I feel caught in a web."

"A spider's web. Oh, the poor thing."

Poor thing indeed. Ambrose, in an effort to distance himself from Pilar, sang like a bird, in Richard's phrase. Vivian had been made to believe she was legally involved in the financial troubles of the foundation and Ambrose had proposed marriage so they could not be called to testify against one another.

"So that is why she played no role in the trial," Katherine said.

Since backing Sancho had gotten him into trouble, Ambrose thought he might get him out too. Of course Sancho knew how to get rich quick—if you already have money, that is. Ambrose actually thought of the cocaine as a business investment.

Some days later they interred Vivian Green's ashes in the hope that now she would be allowed to rest in peace. They adjourned to the house on Walton Street.

"Poor Vivian, to have been caught up with such people," Bridget said.

"A spider's web indeed," Emtee Dempsey said.

"Who gets the coke?" Joyce asked.

"You do," Emtee Dempsey said sternly. "Unless Katherine would prefer a white wine, that is."

A Rose Is a Rose Is a Rose

A Sister Mary Teresa Mystery

1

The roses began to arrive in late February, richly red, long stemmed, three at a time. At mid-morning on Saturday, the truck would pull to the curb outside the house on Walton Street where the remnant of the Order of Martha and Mary lived. A delivery man would scamper up the steps, ring the bell, thrust the roses at Kim or Joyce and say, slowly and distinctly, "A rose is a rose is a rose."

The first time this happened, Joyce had been too stunned even to ask what was meant. Openmouthed, she watched the man run back out to his truck, put it in gear, and ease into the flow of traffic.

"It's obviously a mistake," Sister Mary Teresa Dempsey harumphed when Joyce and Kim stood before her in the study where the elderly nun was busy producing the daily quota of pages that brought her history of the 12th century ever nearer to completion.

"There's a card," Kim observed.

Emtee Dempsey pulled back her head and thrust the roses forward. She still wore the traditional habit of the order and the great starched headdress seemed about to alight on the flowers. "Open it."

Kim opened the little envelope and removed the card.

"A rose is a rose is a rose," she read.

"That's what the man said when he brought them to the door," Joyce said.

"Absurd," said the old nun.

"Gertrude Stein," Kim said.

"Did she sign it?" Joyce asked.

"She wrote it."

"It's typed."

"One would have been sufficient to express identity," Emtee Dempsey said. "A is A. To say A is A is A adds nothing. Of course, the woman was a fraud."

"Maybe she was just counting roses."

It made as much sense as anything else, Kim told Joyce when they had gone into the kitchen to put the flowers in a vase. "What florist was it?"

But Joyce had noticed no name on the truck nor did the card reveal the origin of the roses. Throughout the week, as the roses slowly lost their freshness, Kim imagined the person for whom they had been intended. It seemed a shame that such thoughtfulness should go unknown. What if the misdelivery was the cause of a falling out? But such thoughts dissolved the following Saturday when the second bunch of three long-stemmed roses arrived.

Kim herself answered the bell. It happened so fast. She opened the door, a long box was pressed into her hands as the man said slowly and distinctly, "A rose is a rose is a rose."

The deliveryman looked ordinary enough. The truck at the curb had nothing on its side and there was no legend on the door either.

"What florist are you from?" she demanded.

He looked at her, his expression that of a child who thinks an adult is trying to trick him. He shook his head and without a word ran out to his truck.

"Whoever it is thinks in threes," Emtee Dempsey decided. "The next will be the last."

It was not. Throughout March and into April, on every Saturday without fail, the roses arrived at the door of the house on Walton Street.

"Does one of you have an admirer?" Emtee Dempsey asked, peering first at Joyce and then at Kim.

"They're obviously for you, Sister."

"Obviously?"

"Whoever sends them expects you to understand the message."

"There is nothing to understand."

But even as she said it the old nun's eyes became brighter. Surely she had asked herself the question before this, but never with the intensity she now devoted to the matter.

The scratch of a pen on paper was heard less frequently from the study. Often when Kim looked in, she would see the little nun sitting bolt upright behind her desk, staring fixedly ahead, lost in thought.

"A rose is a rose is a rose," Kim whispered.

Emtee Dempsey said nothing. She did not seem to have heard. Of course she might have been engrossed in some 12th century event, turning it over in her mind before describing it on paper. But Kim was sure that the old nun was thinking that a rose is a rose is a rose.

It angered Kim that she herself wasted hours on the same question, not because she wanted to, but because she could not get it off her mind. If nothing else, the person sending those roses had managed to insinuate himself (herself?) into the consciousness of the house. But it was an annoyed consciousness, a sense of being toyed with.

"Why do you always have such lovely flowers?" Katherine Senski asked one Sunday afternoon when she had dropped by for tea with her old friend Emtee Dempsey.

When Emtee Dempsey, with obvious reluctance, decided that they must not simply pitch the roses out, Joyce had been putting them in less frequented places around the house. The suggestion that they go into the chapel had been vetoed by Emtee Dempsey. God only knew who the donor was and He might not approve of the purpose of the gift. Joyce had put this week's roses in the living room. She might have hoped to prompt the question from Katherine.

"Where did you get those beautiful roses?"

"It's a long story," Emtee Dempsey sighed.

"A story?"

"Sister has a secret admirer," Kim said, and earned a warning glance.

"What Sister Kimberly is putting so facetiously is this."

The old nun's account of what had been happening was crisp, factual and complete, but if she had hoped to make it sound less intriguing, she had failed.

"Every Saturday since February! Did it start on Valentine's Day?"

"It did not."

"It was the last week of the month," Kim said. She and Joyce had long since rejected the Valentine's Day possibility, and with relief. Emtee Dempsey's question to them had raised the unsettling possibility that some man, not realizing that they too were nuns, was making amorous advances. A hurried review had convinced them this could not be the explanation.

Besides, the enigmatic message seemed to point at Emtee Dempsey.

"What have you made of the message?"

"Does it suggest anything to you, Katherine?"

"Something! It suggests a score of things."

Emtee Dempsey put a blank sheet of paper before her and unscrewed her massive fountain pen.

"I will make a list of your suggestions."

Challenged, Katherine faltered. "None of them makes sense."

"We cannot rule out nonsense, Katherine."

Katherine's first guess was the three nuns themselves, then a wine ("Was there an accent?"), then the Cincinnati manager. She went on to ask if Emtee Dempsey had ever had a student named Rose.

"Many of them."

"More than three?"

"Many more than three. And not all of them would be aware of one another."

"But three of them might be."

"I think this is a dead end, Katherine."

"It's just a thought."

Her other suggestions were less helpful still and Emtee Dempsey stopped writing them down.

Katherine sat upright. "I feel as if I'm failing a test."

"The sender has succeeded in annoying everyone then."

"Sister Mary Teresa, you have to think back to when you were a girl. This is clearly a romantic gesture.

"Three roses every Saturday for three months. Does that suggest anything to you?"

"Many things. None of them relevant."

"Some boy?"

"Need I remind you of my age? A boy, as you call him, would now be nearly 80 years old."

"So?"

Emtee Dempsey pursed her lips. That was the end of the conversation, but Katherine's question fed the imaginations of Kim and Joyce. The thought that an ancient boyfriend of

Emtee Dempsey's was now sending her roses, made the Saturday morning delivery almost welcome.

But the first Saturday in April the bell did not ring. No roses were delivered. As if by common consent, no one alluded to it. The game was over, apparently, and it seemed silly to regret it.

At seven that evening the body was found in the truck parked at the curb in front of the house on Walton Street.

2

They had been in the chapel, making a post-prandial visit, when the phone rang. Joyce went into the kitchen to answer it and Kim put her face in her hands to fend off distraction, but soon she was distracted by the fact that, after the phone was picked up, there was no further word from Joyce. Then there was the sound of the front door opening. Emtee Dempsey, kneeling at her prie-dieu just ahead of Kim, seemed oblivious to this. Had Joyce left the house? Five minutes went by and then again the sound of the front door and of Joyce running through the house. She stood in the chapel door. Waiting. But the old nun was still sunk in prayer.

"There's a body out front!" Joyce finally cried out.

A minute later, Emtee Dempsey stood on the front porch while Kim and Joyce went out to the parked truck. The woman behind the wheel might have been caught up in some sort of meditational trance, like Emtee Dempsey only moments before. Or she might simply have been drunk like a significant percentage of the avenue's habitués. Finally the old nun came out to the truck. Traffic began to react confusedly when the short and wide figure in the fantastic garb appeared in the street. Emtee Dempsey stood for a full minute looking in at the woman and then returned to the walk and permitted them to help her up the steps to the door.

"Call the cathedral rectory, Sister Joyce." A great puffing sigh as she made it onto the porch. She paused before continuing. "And the police, of course. Call the police as well."

A squad car came, arriving only a minute before Father Maloney who administered the sacraments with a sad look on his pocked face. Later in the study, he assured Emtee Dempsey the woman had gone to judgment without benefit of clergy.

"I never heard the phrase used that way before."

Maloney, not familiar with all the nuances of the old nun's voice, took this as a compliment.

Richard Moriarty, Kim's brother and a detective lieutenant with the Chicago police, entered the house with a frown, seemingly certain that his old nemesis was once more creating trouble for him.

"What do you know about it?" he demanded when they were all seated in Emtee Dempsey's study. He was less frowny now, having accepted Joyce's offer of a beer. Kim didn't particularly like the idea that her brother's good will could be had for the price of a bottle of beer.

"I know what Father Maloney has told me."

"Maloney?"

"He gave her the last sacraments."

"When?"

"He knew at the time she was dead."

"She has been dead at least twelve hours," Richard said, perhaps rejecting the notion that the priest had special powers of discernment.

"Good heavens."

"She was holding a bouquet of flowers."

"What do you make of that?" the old nun asked.

"They're not the kind kids hawk in bars, the outer petals torn off, wrapped in wax paper. These are first class roses. Still fresh."

"Thoughtful," the old nun murmured.

"Yeah. You got another of these?" he asked Joyce, flourishing his glass.

"Come back when you're off duty, Richard," Kim said, with an edge to her voice. God created whisky so the Irish wouldn't rule the world, and beer is no better, as her father had always added.

"And bring your lovely wife," Emtee Dempsey said brightly, rising to her feet.

Richard had little choice but to go. If he had been offering rather than seeking information the old nun would have emptied the refrigerator of beer for him. When he was gone, she said, "Call Katherine and see if she can come at once. Don't tell her what happened unless it's necessary to induce her to come."

Katherine needed no excuse for a visit to Walton Street. She was not as frequent a visitor as she might be only because she dreaded imposing on their hospitality and making a nuisance of herself. So far as the three nuns were concerned, Katherine could have a room on the second floor, or take the basement apartment, and stay permanently if she wanted, but like many elderly single women Katherine cherished her independence even more than she craved the companionship of old friends.

"Were flowers delivered today?" she asked when they were comfortable in the living room. Joyce pushed the tea trolley up next to the old nun's chair and waited to carry cups. Kim and Katherine sat on the facing sofas that flanked the fireplace.

"No, Katherine, not flowers. At least not only flowers."

"Don't tease me."

"A dead body too."

Katherine's hands flew up. "You're not serious."

Emtee Dempsey was perfectly content to tell Katherine what they knew, because she intended to ask her a favor.

"I want you to check on the woman's recent background."

"Do the police know who she is?"

"No."

Katherine looked at Kim and then up at Joyce who was putting a cup of tea in her hands.

"How would you suggest I check on her?"

"I think I know who it is. Or was."

3

The body discovered in the truck parked in front of the house on Walton Street had been the mortal coil shuffled off by Barbara Selton, aged forty-seven. Nothing found on the body indicated this, but a glance through the truck window had sufficed to stir Emtee Dempsey's memory. With that lead, Katherine Senski had a good head start on the police and she used it to advantage.

Barbara Selton, a native of Ottumwa, Iowa had attended Knox College and then come on to Chicago to do graduate work in English. She had received a master's from the University of Chicago after four years of study. Armed with that and enrolled at Loyola, she continued work toward the doctorate while teaching part time at the college then operated by the Order of Martha and Mary west of the city.

"She was not a successful teacher," Emtee Dempsey recalled. "The girls were merciless with her, urging her to declaim poetry by the page, the better to get through her classes."

"How long did she teach?" Katherine asked.

"You wonder why we did not let her go. The reason is both simple and crass. She came cheap. Part-time teachers are paid but a fraction of a regular salary. Barbara was economical for us. These were the beginning of the bad years, Katherine. Financially. Not that Barbara was incompetent. Far from it. True, she had difficulty completing her graduate studies, but she was zealous. Once I was impressed to hear a student reciting John Donne's 'The Anniversarie' only to learn that she was mimicking poor Barbara Selton. She was not a prepossessing person."

When Kim thought of the woman seated behind the wheel of the parked truck, it was her own horror she recalled at the realization that it was death she stared at. The face had seemed so small because of the hair—a wig, as it turned out—and the intensity of her expression as she stared sightlessly ahead seemed to gather the narrow face into the forward thrust of her arched nose. The jogging costume in which she was found seemed to explain the fact that there was not a spare ounce on her.

"She jogged religiously every day," Katherine said, trying to make her voice neutral.

"Twice a day," said the maintenance man at the building in which Barbara Selton had lived with her mother and brother. He shook his head. "Six-thirty a.m., she came out of that elevator, up that ramp and was on her way. Twelve hours later, same thing. Every day. Like a clock."

"She should have been healthy to a fault," Emtee Dempsey said. "What did she die of?"

"Asphyxiation," Richard said.

The truck she was found in had been reported missing by

Aronstein Delivery. Barbara had not died at the wheel. There was evidence that she had been held captive in the back of the truck and that she had died there. At the Aronstein garage, hoses were attached to the exhaust pipes of trucks whose motors were running inside the building, diverting it outside. There was evidence that such a hose had been taped to an air vent on the side of the truck.

"A mobile death camp," the old nun said.

Richard thought about that, but said nothing. "She must have been put behind the wheel after the truck was brought here."

Was that possible? Of course it was. Anything was possible on a city street. Passersby had trained themselves not to notice things. Besides, who would have imagined the woman was dead. She might have been drunk. Or ill. But dead? Even on Walton Street that would have seemed farfetched.

"Do you know who she was?" Sister Mary Teresa asked this with a straight face.

Kim got up and went into the kitchen where Joyce was watching the Cubs on a diminutive television set. She asked what was up but she didn't pay very close attention when Kim told her. The game was in the seventh; a scoreless tie and the foe had the bases loaded with one out. Well, Kim could hardly expect Joyce to be as indignant as she was because Emtee Dempsey was misleading Richard. Whoever had killed Barbara Selton could benefit from withholding such information. It was unfair and probably illegal not to tell Richard who the woman had been.

"Don't worry about the murderer escaping," Emtee Dempsey said. "I consider it a matter of honor to apprehend him. The idea, leaving a body at our doorstep." She did not mention the roses that had been found with the woman, but it was an unspoken conviction in the house on Walton Street that there was a connection between the mysterious delivery of roses and the death of Barbara Selton.

"Why do you say him?" Katherine asked.

"I use the pronoun generically. Would you prefer that I said him or her?"

"At the *Tribune* now we must."

But the usual expostulation was not forthcoming from the old nun. She looked across the room thoughtfully, but what she saw was not here.

"Barbara Selton was punctilious about grammar. It was another bone of contention with the students. Whenever she read exams or other papers, she was ruthless in taking off for grammatical mistakes."

"But you were the same."

"I trust that Barbara Selton and I were not alone in thinking that college students should be proficient in their native language. But she had a way of antagonizing as well as correcting."

"That sounds like her reviews."

"Reviews?"

"Nothing grand. She reviewed books occasionally for a west-side shoppers' guide."

"Tell me about her family."

This was addressed to Kim who had visited Barbara's mother after Emtee Dempsey had agreed to inform Richard of the identity of the murdered woman.

The three nuns went to the wake, out of genuine sympathy of course at the death of one of Sister Mary Teresa's former colleagues, but it served to break the ice as well, if that was the appropriate expression. Victor Selton and his mother seemed frozen in something worse than ice. The mother could not have been Emtee Dempsey's age, but she sat hunched in her chair, gripping a cane as if she might soon do an acrobatic trick with it. Kim could not resist the thought that Mrs. Selton resembled a monkey peering out at the strange creatures that had come to visit her. Not that Kasnieski's Funeral Home was her regular cage, although she seemed to belong there, but she looked up while keeping her chin down and this gave her the expression of a somewhat coquettish rhesus. Victor stood behind the winged chair in which his mother sat, looking over it warily at Emtee Dempsey.

"Your daughter taught at our college," the old nun was shouting at Mrs. Selton.

No answer.

"She taught English and was much remarked on by the students." The old nun's voice lifted even higher, as she tried to elicit a response from the little dark eyes that looked up at her through a fringe of grizzled brows.

Emtee Dempsey inhaled, but before she could speak again, Mrs. Selton spoke.

"I'm not deaf."

"Thank God for that."

"It's Victor."

"I beg your pardon."

"My son Victor is deaf. From firecrackers when he was a boy. My daughter was murdered."

The old nun took Mrs. Selton's hand and patted it. "Let us think of her as with God."

"She didn't believe in God."

"God believes in her."

"She would have a fit if she knew I let them have this." The hand slipped free of Emtee Dempsey's and indicated the viewing room. "A rosary. Mass tomorrow."

"You did the right thing. People sometimes say skeptical things and don't mean them."

"She called herself an atheist. She went on and on about it. The proof was evil."

She meant that her daughter had considered God's existence incompatible with evil in the world. Emtee Dempsey pulled a chair next to the old woman's and began to discourse on the problem of evil. It was absurd, but it made as much sense as anything else. Three or four people from their neighborhood came and that is all.

"We only moved to Chicago ten years ago."

"To be with your daughter?"

"She needed a home."

This enigmatic remark meant, as Kim was to discover three days later, that Mrs. Selton had brought with her the proceeds from selling her house in Ottumwa plus her husband's insurance money, had bought the modest house in sight of the Dan Ryan Expressway. It was one of those sad little streets Kim had often glimpsed from the expressway, usually in winter when they were clogged with snow. There was something pathetic about them, scrunched together, studies in fading grays and browns. Mrs. Selton was proud to be the owner of Chicago real estate—she had been assured it was a good investment—but to Kim it seemed a modest holding. Victor sat at the dining room table while she talked with his mother.

"Losing his sister must be very difficult for Victor."

"They did nothing but fight."

"Where did Barbara work?"

"Work! Neither of them worked. When she wasn't running through the streets in that silly costume she was in the back room writing."

"Writing?"

"She tried to write dirty novels." This from Victor, whose voice was surprisingly bass. It startled Kim to have him enter the conversation; she had assumed he couldn't hear a word.

"He reads lips. Test him."

Victor turned from his mother and actually grinned at Kim. He nodded. Kim felt like a fool, mouthing the words.

"No more taxes!" Victor cried, and even his mother laughed.

Something moved on the floor near the fireplace and Kim realized it was a dog. A huge dog. It stood, dipped in a prolonged stretch, then turned its head and regarded Kim. The head turned slowly away and then the dog slumped back onto the floor.

"Did Barbara publish anything?"

Victor shook his head. "They always came back."

While Kim was wondering what their reaction would be if she asked to see some of Barbara's work, Victor said in his loud voice, "You want to see some?"

He led her down a narrow ill-lit hall to a corner room, standing aside so that she could look inside. The drapes were pulled, the room was dark except for the green glow of a computer monitor.

"She always leaves it on. They told her always to leave it on."

How eerie to think that days after Barbara had died her computer stood in readiness here. Victor darted into the room and came back with a rectangular box.

"She'd kill me for showing you this."

They went back to Mrs. Selton and Kim spent the rest of the visit with the box on her lap, half expecting Victor to ask for it back. She had lifted the cover and looked at the top page. *Needy Blood* by Barbara Dempsey. Dempsey!

"Did Barbara ever publish anything?"

"She wrote for the shoppers' guide," Mrs. Selton said. She seemed unsure whether to be proud of this.

"Did she ever publish a book?"

Victor's high tuneless laughter was the answer to that.

If the old woman and her stone deaf son had moved to Chicago in order to be with Barbara—something their behavior rendered somewhat dubious—there was nothing to prevent their returning to Ottumwa now. Of course Kim did not bring it up, but back in Walton Street she put the question.

Emtee Dempsey asked if she were suggesting a motive.

"Their behavior is odd but there is little doubt their lives revolved around Barbara's. Her room is the centerpiece of the house, particularly now when she is no longer in it. The neighbors may have found her eccentric, a determined old maid, but they all speak of her with respect, even affection. The only one who would seem to have a reason to kill her is one of those old students of hers you spoke of."

"That's nonsense."

"I know."

"Do you intend to read that novel?"

"I brought it home for you."

Emtee Dempsey sighed. She preferred old novels, and gloried a bit in the contradiction—novels were by definition new.

"Barbara Dempsey!" the old nun cried when she had lifted the cover of the box containing Barbara Selton's novel.

"You have no idea how many you have influenced," Katherine said with glee. "Besides, you can't expect her to publish a dirty novel under her own name."

"I have no expectations one way or the other, Katherine. This is amusing. I will grant you that." Emtee Dempsey did not sound in the least bit amused. "But I was struck by another name in this matter."

Kim and Joyce and Katherine waited. It could be a risky thing to take up Sister Mary Teresa when she uttered such enigmatic statements.

"Aronstein," she murmured, as if to herself.

They waited. The truck in which Barbara had been found dead was stolen from Aronstein's Delivery. Neither Katherine nor the police had discovered any relationship at all between Barbara and the delivery service. Unable to maintain her prudent silence, Katherine reminded Emtee Dempsey of this.

"Yes, yes. But think of the name. Think of the rose."

Kim said, "Gertrude Stein."

"Of course. The same number of syllables, accent on the penultimate. Clearly it was meant to suggest the author of 'A rose is a rose is a rose.' We might overlook this if the roses Barbara was found with did not connect her death with our mysterious admirer."

Kim was grateful her brother Richard was not there to hear this uncharacteristically fanciful parlay on the part of Sister Mary Teresa. The only thing to commend her guess was that it made as little sense as the events it was meant to connect.

4

The funeral for Barbara Selton, doubtless due to the newspaper publicity, attracted a crowd, but far from disturbing Mrs. Selton and Victor, the bereaved seemed delighted with the turnout. Surely they must have realized that the pews were filled with the morbid, gawkers, the merely curious.

St. Romuald's church recalled better times in the neighborhood in which it stood. Many dioceses would have delighted to have the church for their cathedral. It was a vast Romanesque structure but oddly proportioned, almost as wide as it was long. The arrangement of the pews suggested a cruciform building, but this was not the case. Indeed, the location of the altar at the point where four banks of pews converged from the east, west, south and north was due to a post-Vatican II remodeling of the church. This had occurred just prior to the flight to the suburbs that had left St. Romouald's a bare, if not unruined choir. Thus it was easily able to accommodate the crowd that turned out for the woman whose murder had entertained Chicagoans for several days. That Richard had picked Howard Wren out of such a multitude was remarkable. But then Howard Wren had come to the cemetery as well.

"Who is Richard talking to?" Emtee Dempsey whispered to Kim. They were seated on folding chairs across from Mrs. Selton and Victor. Between them was the open grave and, mounted above it on the lowering device, the coffin containing the remains of Barbara. Father Maloney was fighting a generally successful battle with the fresh breeze that tried to turn the pages of his book before he completed his reading.

Richard was clearly visible on an angle to their right. His hand held the upper arm of a tall bald man in what might have been an official grip. The man had leaned toward Richard, frowning as he listened. He turned and cocked his head in a birdlike way before nodding. Richard let go of his arm and folded his own, a most non-funereal smile on his face.

Kim tried to let a shrug suffice for an answer but eventually had to whisper to Emtee Dempsey that she did not know. Father Maloney was put off more by this whispering than he was by the wind. But soon he was sprinkling the casket with holy water.

163

"It is absurd not to complete the burial while the bereaved are at graveside."

"It is almost never done now, Sister," Katherine said.

"Are the relatives supposed to be capable of viewing the corpse, seeing the freshly dug hole and then unable to see the body lowered to its final rest?"

"I'm not defending it, Sister, simply stating a fact."

Kim waited for this exchange to complete itself. Richard had stayed close to the tall bald man when the ceremony was over, but he acted as if he were alone when Kim came up to him. But she had been sent on a mission and she meant to complete it. She thrust out her hand.

"I'm Sister Kimberly. Richard's sister."

"You're a nun? Of course you are. I see the veil." He made this sound like an accomplishment, but then anything compared with Emtee Dempsey's headdress would seem invisible. "Do you know the little old nun who was seated beside the grave?"

"Sister Mary Teresa? We live in the same house."

"I thought that's who it must be."

"Are you a relative?"

He explained that he was not. His name was Howard Wren. Richard had been patient throughout this interruption, but when Kim suggested that Howard Wren come meet Sister Mary Teresa now, Richard drew the line.

"Mr. Wren has agreed to come with me."

"Under arrest!" Wren emitted a chirping little laugh. If he was worried, he didn't show it.

"Come see us," Kim urged. "We live on Walton Street."

"But who is Howard Wren?" Emtee Dempsey asked when Kim reported this. The old nun turned to Katherine, but the reporter shrugged her padded shoulders.

On the drive home, Joyce told Kim that the Seltons had

been invited for lunch. That had been thoughtful and any dismay Kim felt at the suggestion that she had somehow failed in her mission disappeared.

Emtee Dempsey herself took the old woman and her son on a tour of the house. Designed by Frank Lloyd Wright, it had been designated a national monument.

"Unlike its occupants," she added.

Victor moved his own lips as he read the old nun's but that didn't help. Emtee Dempsey devoted several minutes to trying to explain her little joke and then gave up. It took some of the zest from her role as hostess. But Victor redeemed himself at the table when Emtee Dempsey mentioned the presence of Howard Wren at the funeral. She said it as if everyone in the world knew who Howard Wren was. The Seltons certainly did.

"Howard Wren," the old woman cried. "After all these years."

"How long has it been?"

"Oh, I never met him. Why didn't he come say hello."

"We were still in Ottumwa," Victor said. "Barbara made it sound like there'd be a wedding. At least that's the way mother took it."

"She had never spoken of any other man like that."

"Because no one else had ever taken her out."

"That's not true!"

"I mean after she moved to Chicago."

The time of this liaison coincided with that during which Barbara had been teaching at the college, but when Emtee Dempsey professed surprise—after the Seltons were gone—that she had been unaware of the young man's attentions, Katherine permitted herself to wonder if her old friend would (a) have been interested in the romantic life of a part-time teacher and (b) whether she would have recognized the seriousness of the relationship.

"Relationship," Emtee Dempsey repeated, but stopped herself from commenting on the use to which this abstract term has lately been put. "I do of course defer to you on such matters, Katherine. But clearly the matter is of interest to the police."

This all but overt reference to the grand doomed passion of Katherine Senski's life was unusual for Emtee Dempsey and had not been meant to cause her old friend pain in any way. What clearly interested her was the interest Richard had shown in Howard Wren.

Katherine said, "I don't see what I could find out about him, Sister. I mean about his connection with Barbara Selton. Unless they announced their engagement."

After what Victor had said that was unlikely and indeed it had not been announced, more likely than not because it had not happened. Victor seemed to relish emphasizing this.

"The boy always taunted Barbara about the fish that got away."

"The bird," Victor corrected. "The bird. His name is Wren."

"Like the great architect. Sister, I love your house."

Kim drove the mother and son back to their own house, helped the old woman inside and accepted her invitation to come in. In the living room, Mrs. Selton hunched forward, gripping her cane. "Now that Barbara is gone I see no reason to remain in Chicago. I want to go back to Ottumwa to die."

"That's the only thing there is to do there," Victor said.

"Not the only thing, Victor. You were born there."

"But where was I conceived?"

"Victor! You go to your room at once."

He rose without protest, a man in his late thirties,

punished by his mother like a schoolboy.

"Did he often tease Barbara?"

"In self-defense. Of course she had the advantage."

"How so?"

"If she spoke from another room or when he couldn't read her lips, she could get away with anything."

The old woman laughed but there were tears in her eyes. Did she miss those scenes of domestic bliss? Five minutes later, she was regretting that Victor was no longer with them.

"Should I call him?"

"He wouldn't hear you."

Kim could scarcely offer to go to the "boy's" room and fetch him.

"Well, I can tell you what Victor told me. A man called about Barbara's writing. He is interested in it and would like to see anything she did."

"A publisher?"

"No, he called himself an agent."

Mrs. Selton was delighted, but then she had seen nothing ghoulish in the large number that had turned out for the funeral. Emtee Dempsey's reaction, when told of this, was similar to Kim's.

"Is this what literature has become? The cynical exploitation of news events? I suppose from a commercial point of view, it wouldn't matter a great deal that Barbara Selton simply lacked the gift for writing credible fiction. *Needy Blood* may not be the dirty novel her brother imagines it to be, but it is an obscenity nonetheless. It seems to be deliberately bad. I cannot believe that Barbara was not capable of something better than this."

"If it's bad enough, it could become a bestseller."

Kim disputed this theory of literary success, but Katherine

and Emtee Dempsey pointed out that she was the one who had brought the news that a literary agent had expressed interest.

"What is his name?"

"I don't know. His mother sent Victor to his room and he wasn't there to answer such questions."

"You needn't be facetious, Sister."

Kim explained that she was being quite literal. The old nun shook her head as Kim described the scene at the Seltons.

"Imagine someone marrying into a menage like that. No wonder Howard Wren took flight."

"Sister, we have no idea how serious that was."

"That is why I must see Howard Wren."

5

"He's looking better all the time," Richard said, when Emtee Dempsey asked him about Howard Wren.

"In what way?"

Richard tipped his glass and contemplated the beer that remained in it. Emtee Dempsey shamelessly offered him another and Richard shamelessly accepted and Kim, to her shame, was sent to fetch it.

"Why begrudge the man a beer?" Joyce asked.

"A beer? This is his second. Besides, drink runs in my family."

"Like blood?"

"Almost. I've told you of my Uncle Dan. Richard even looks like him. I hate to see him drink."

"Beer isn't drinking."

"That's what my Aunt Eloise always said, until the hallucinations began."

"Ye gods. Better bring him a root beer."

"Do we have any?"

"I'll buy some."

In the meantime, Richard could have his second beer. Kim could see that Joyce thought she was exaggerating her fears, and she was, but better to exaggerate beforehand than afterward.

"But, Richard," Emtee Dempsey was saying, "lots of people jog."

"Every day? And taking pretty much the same route Barbara Selton took?"

"A coincidence."

"Uh uh." Richard accepted the beer without so much as a by-your-leave. "On purpose."

"But they hadn't seen one another for years."

"It was the route they jogged together in the sweet by and by. He quit for years and just went back to it six months ago. He said it was half conscious, running their old route, but now he sees that was the reason he chose it, out of fond memories."

"Of jogging with Barbara?"

Richard nodded.

"I won't insult you by telling you how farfetched that is. You must have solider reason for suspecting Howard Wren."

"He's not a suspect!" Richard cried. "I am relying on your discretion not to mention this."

To Kim it was clear that this was one investigation Richard felt so far ahead on that he could indulge himself and let the old nun into the results of solid police work.

Kim said, "We're always dragging policemen in here, plying them with drink and then getting all their secrets out of them."

Richard defiantly tossed off half a glass of beer. But he spoke to Emtee Dempsey.

"You're right. There is something more."

"What?"

"I wish I could tell you."

"Richard Moriarity, that is unfair. You can't tease an old woman in this way. What in the world harm can it do if an old nun knows a little of what you have learned?"

Rather than being made wary by this patently disingenuous remark, Richard smiled as if reassured and went on.

"He made inquiries with a private detective on how he might locate Barbara."

"He told you that?"

"Let's say it came out in the course of our interview. I don't think he fully realized how significant that is."

"Which suggests that it means nothing. I mean nothing so far as your investigation goes."

"Oh, he emphasized that he had never gone through with it. The man he talked with is an old guy named Puller. He talked to Puller several times. Puller thinks he was just trying to find out how to locate Barbara Selton on his own."

"And you think he did?"

"It's possible. And then he took up jogging. Maybe they met, he tried to get things back the way they used to be, she told him to buzz off and . . ."

"Richard, when you retire, you must take up fiction. Everyone is. Did you know Barbara Selton wrote a novel?"

But Richard took offense at the suggestion that he was telling a story rather than reciting facts. He even left half of his second bottle of beer undrunk when he left.

"Keep us posted," Emtee Dempsey urged him.

"On the progress of my fiction?"

"Now, Richard."

He stooped and kissed Emtee Dempsey on the cheek, a sign of magnanimity on his part, and embarrassing for the old nun. She had noted the sudden vogue of kissing all and sundry and considered it the trivialization of something important.

"But Sister," Kim said, amused by the old nun's embarrassment. "Most forms of greeting are trivilizations of something. The handshake is a checking for weapons, goodbye a carryover from religious times. God be with you."

"Gruss Gott, as Blessed Abigail Keineswegs was wont to say. You're absolutely right and Richard is a dear. I don't know why you badger him so."

Kim was deeply engaged in defending herself before she realized how Emtee Dempsey had switched the field on her. She must learn not to tease the old nun. Invariably it turned out that it was Kim rather than Emtee Dempsey who was on the run.

The following day, after they returned from Mass at the cathedral, Kim was on the run literally. It was seven, slightly later than when Barbara Selton had done her morning jog and Kim had the sense of running against the current of the rest of the world which was on its way to work. If Barbara had noticed this, she might have been unbothered by it. She worked at home, however, and was unlikely to have felt guilt. Emtee Dempsey wanted a firsthand report on what it was like to jog in Chicago. She took the route Barbara had. It had been publicized in the news and Kim had the idea that the media had made jogging along that path chic among semi-psychopathic sensation seekers. For that matter, she herself felt eerie running this route. It was impossible not to think of Barbara, dutifully pumping along this very path in Grant Park. If Howard Wren knew the path of Barbara's run he could have acquired it by reading the newspapers in the days after her body was found.

And then she saw him. He was unmistakable, bone thin,

six foot three, the multicolored sweatband emphasizing his hairless pate. He ran with loose-jointed ease, without the grimace that identified the neophyte or obsessive runner. He seemed to be hardly moving but it took Kim two hundred yards to catch up with him and that meant racing rather than jogging so that when she came up beside him she hardly had breath to say hello.

His height varied between its normal and considerably more as he ran, but from either elevation he looked down at her with some surprise.

"Could we talk?"

He thought about it for some twenty yards then shrugged.

"I meant could we stop."

He frowned but then he looked at her again and Kim realized he had just recognized her. But of course it was silly to think he would know her, done up in Joyce's Notre Dame sweatsuit and wearing a White Sox cap. ("Joyce, it will get ruined." "That's what I had in mind." "You know you love the Sox." "It's not reciprocated," Joyce said with disgust. The White Sox were once more in the cellar of the weakest division in the major leagues. "Go ahead, wear it. It is a perfect disguise.") Kim had forgotten how unrecognizable she was.

"Sister!" Howard Wren finally cried, causing heads to turn.

"Call me Kimberly."

"This is a surprise. I didn't know nuns jogged." More heads turned but Howard Wren had stopped, sort of. He ran in place, bounding up and down, his knees rising and falling like pistons. Kim just stopped, removing the Sox cap.

"Keep moving," Howard warned. "Your muscles will tighten up."

It seemed the lesser of two evils, the worst being that she

might simply die. Joyce would have been perfect for this errand, as Joyce herself had pointed out, but Emtee Dempsey had made up her mind. Now that she had met Howard Wren, Kim was glad she was there, although not glad about the running.

"I'm out of breath."

"You'll get a second wind."

"I don't have a first."

It was clear he did not intend to stop moving. How could he make it look so effortless?

"Come see us," Kim said.

"I've tried. I didn't know what to look under." He meant in the phone book. No wonder he hadn't found them. They were listed as The Order of Martha and Mary. Sister Mary Teresa refused to accept their present diminished condition as final and was fond of reminding them that Our Lord began with only twelve. To which the answer was that only one of the twelve had deserted, whereas the Order of Martha and Mary had lost all but the three of them. Kim gave this puffing information to Howard Wren who continued to go up and down as if on a pogo stick.

"What on earth is a pogo stick?" Emtee Dempsey asked later.

"It doesn't matter."

But Joyce began to describe it and, infuriatingly, Emtee Dempsey encouraged her to go again. If she was delighted that Kim had had the good luck of encountering Howard Wren while jogging in Grant Park, she was disguising it better than the baseball cap had Kim.

"He'll be coming to see us."

"Good."

"Sister Mary Teresa, you were the one who asked him to come. I was merely repeating your invitation."

"Your brother seems to have gotten everything out of him already."

So that's what it was. Emtee Dempsey never quite admitted that she had a bad habit of competing with the police in the person of Kim's brother, but her reaction now was better—worse, rather—than an admission. She had been interested in Howard Wren when there was a chance that she would find out what Richard now had. In the same way, she had not informed Richard when she verified that the body in the truck did indeed belong to Barbara Selton. It was a moment when Kim would have fully justified in engaging in what Emtee Dempsey called fraternal correction, pointing out to her that she was being childish. But she was not without sin herself. She wanted the old nun to acknowledge that she had been lucky to run into Howard Wren and resourceful in insuring that he would be coming to the house on Walton Street.

"Sister," she said, "you know you will be able to learn more from one conversation with Howard Wren than the police have in all their investigations."

That was a mistake. If there was one thing the old nun was not susceptible to, it was flattery. Kim knew it was a mistake even as she said it. All the remark did was confirm Emtee Dempsey in her indifference to the impending visit of Howard Wren.

"I'll tell you the person I would like to see."

Kim said nothing but summoned up a receptive expression that cost her much.

"The literary agent who expressed interest in Barbara's writing."

Of all the perverse diversions imaginable, this seemed the worst to Kim. How like Emtee Dempsey to express interest in such a peripheral figure.

"How about the mailman?" Kim asked.

"The mailman?"

"The one who brought back all Barbara Selton's rejected manuscripts. He might be able to cast light on what happened."

But the old nun refused to take the remark as ironic. "A very Chestertonian suggestion, Sister. I will keep it in mind. But first things first. Now I would like to speak to that agent."

"Maybe Howard Wren's detective could find him."

"Mr. Puller? Yes, I thought of that. But he seemed eager to tell everything to Richard, didn't he? I think we would be better advised to proceed on our own. Besides, as your manner suggests, this is a very remote possibility indeed."

6

Victor might be deaf but Kim felt dumb calling again on the Seltons. It was the first time that it dawned on her that Victor lived the life of a retired man, although he was not yet forty. Had he ever worked? His occupation seemed to be companion of his widowed mother and, until recently, relentless gadfly to his older sister. What a menage the three of them must have made. For that matter, what a menage Mrs. Selton and Victor continued to make.

"How do you know someone is at the door?" she asked Victor. His concentration on her lips made her pronounce words in an exaggerated way.

"Because I tell him," called Mrs. Selton from the sitting room. The television was audible there and Kim thought of all the programs that had a cameo screen in which someone translated the speaker into sign language.

"Do you know sign language?" she asked Victor.

His brow darkened and he shook his head. "It's only good with other deaf people."

He referred to the deaf in disdain. In the living room, fitfully as commercials came on, Mrs. Selton explained that Victor's deafness was not congenital but had been brought on by an explosion when he was eight years old.

"He was a very bright child. More so than Barbara had been."

"I only lost my hearing, not my mind," Victor corrected.

"God knows you kept your pride. Victor is very angry about his handicap."

"Handicap! I'm deaf. I can't hear. You make me sound like a golfer."

Kim could not tell whether the exchanges between mother and son were arguments or playful badinage or an unstable mixture of both. This must have been a very electric apartment when Barbara was here to contribute her two cents worth. In any case, the point of Mrs. Selton's story was that Victor was educated at home more than at school, her late husband tutoring the boy and catering to his natural gifts. And Victor had taught himself. He was an omnivorous reader, never watched television, was indeed a gentleman of leisure. His mother was fortunate, more or less, to have Victor at her beck and call. It was a nice question who was looking after whom.

"I wanted to ask a few questions about Barbara's writing."

"Victor can help you there," the old woman said, effectively dismissing them.

In the kitchen, Victor poured coffee and they sat at the table. It was not unlike talking with Joyce in the kitchen of the house on Walton Street.

"Have you read her novel?" Victor asked.

"Not yet."

He grinned. "Meaning you took a peek and couldn't bear the thought."

"No. Meaning that Sister Mary Teresa is reading it first."

"I'd like to know what she thinks of it."

"You'll have to ask her."

The suggestion made him uneasy, as if he were as reluctant to go out as the old nun was. She left the house at least once a day, in order to go to Mass, but so far as Kim could see Victor never went out. He confirmed this when she asked.

"Not even on weekends?"

"I do take mother to church."

"But Barbara didn't go with?"

"Sister, I'll be frank. I take my mother; I do not go myself. I get through it by going into a meditative trance."

"Church is a good place for that."

"Barbara's crude argument from the existence of evil could be easily dealt with by a theist. But no one can touch a solipsist rejection and it is to that I subscribe."

"Solipsist?"

She was sorry she asked five minutes later when he was still sketching his theory that Victor Selton was the only thing in existence, the world and other people a projection of his mind. There was no God in that world.

"In order to refute me one must in effect argue that I have a pain I do not feel."

No wonder Mrs. Selton preferred the television. That Victor was bright, extremely bright, was obvious enough, but even in this effort to establish his deepest unbeliefs, he seemed to be playing a game, pretending, not quite serious. How different Sister Mary Teresa was. However much she enjoyed the give and take of dialectic, she never forgot that the mind is made for truth, a truth it does not itself make.

"But back to Barbara's writing," Kim said.

"I have been trying to spare you. Barbara had no talent, no creative talent. As a critic, she had her merit."

"*Needy Blood* doesn't seem to be very ambitious."

He shook his head. "Why did she sink so low? I can't tell you. She lacked the talent for trash just as she lacked the talent for literature. She was meant to complete her doctorate and retail literature to disinterested youth. She could do no harm, she might do a little good, and it would have gotten her out from under mother's feet."

"And yours?"

"Please don't misunderstand. As an adversary, Barbara was without peer."

She had also been the only one to whom Victor could really talk. Kim realized that he would keep her here for hours if only to vent his own theories.

"You said that an agent inquired about her work?"

"Of course mother took the call. I wrote down the message for Barbara."

"Do you remember his name?"

"No. It was difficult to take seriously."

"But Barbara did get the message."

"My note may still be in her room. Would you like to look?"

The computer continued to run. Kim might have imagined it to be a species of vigil light if she hadn't come to know Victor. He remained on the threshold while she looked on the desktop for the note. Clearly Barbara was a saver. On her desk things rose like layers of lasagna in a complete absence of system or order. From the doorway Victor urged her to rummage around and Kim did, confident now that any note Barbara had been given Barbara would have kept. She did not find the note, but she found something better. It was a letter expressing interest in her work. The stationery was that of a New York Literary Agency, Adam Pieta Associates. It was dated two years earlier.

"Was the call from Adam Pieta?"

She had to repeat the name but no recognition shone in Victor's eyes. "Maybe mother will remember."

Mrs. Selton did not even remember but gave Kim permission to take the letter with her. Driving back to Walton Street Kim felt a childish disappointment to match that of which she accused Emtee Dempsey. If the old nun was pursuing the literary agent spoor just to be contrary, because she was unwilling to concede that the police investigation centering on Howard Wren was indeed plausible. Kim herself was disappointed that she had apparently found the name of the agent, thus feeding the old nun's contrariness. Kim had little doubt that very shortly she would be placing a call to the offices of Adam Pieta in New York.

Which is why the sight of Richard's car parked in front of the house on Walton Street struck her as a reprieve. And indeed there was a triumphant expression on his face.

"I've just come to bring Howard Wren's excuses. At his request. He couldn't make it himself."

"They have arrested Howard Wren," Sister Mary Teresa said, her tone the one she might have used to tell Kim someone had denied the unity of the human race.

"Two and two have a way of making four."

Surely Richard wasn't always this smug. He was reacting to Emtee Dempsey, just as she herself sometimes did, and it did no good to invoke the childish excuse that the old nun had started it. She at least had been corrupted by always being right. Until now. It was undeniable that the case against Howard Wren was strong. Richard ticked off the points.

"First, they had once been quite close and then broke up. Second, there is reason to think he never accepted this. He lived close by Barbara Selton, he jogged the same route she did every day, a sentimental choice. By the way, Kim, you were seen jogging that route."

"By whom?" She was embarrassed to think of herself in that absurd costume. Besides, she ached all over from the exertion. Whatever the attractions of jogging, they eluded her. Joyce had begged her not to complain as she hoped to get permission to jog regularly, if not every day. Kim promised nothing. It would be like Emtee Dempsey to require that they jog together, belatedly finding the thought of a nun out jogging alone unacceptable.

"Did Howard Wren inform you?" Emtee Dempsey asked.

"As a matter of fact, he hasn't mentioned it. That doesn't surprise me, of course. He is not what you would call candid, Sister. No, you were observed by policemen on duty."

"Don't tell me O'Connell and Gleason were jogging!"

Richard laughed. "I wish I'd thought of that. They did have the area under surveillance. Add it up. Wren has been nursing a passion, more likely a grudge, for years. He has lived in his present apartment two years. He jogs where the deceased jogged. Far too much there for coincidence."

"Barbara was accosted while jogging at night."

"That's right."

"Howard Wren jogged in the morning. Did he also jog at night?"

"Twice a day?"

"Barbara Selton jogged twice a day. You will probably find Howard Wren as surprised as you are to learn that Barbara always jogged at night."

"Nothing Wren affirms or denies carries much weight with me, Sister Mary Teresa."

It was painful to Kim to listen to Emtee Dempsey play with so weak a hand. Why couldn't she accept Howard Wren as the principal suspect? He was the only suspect. Everything she asked in an effort to disturb Richard's assumption served to strengthen it.

"Has he told you of his love of poetry?"

Richard shook his head.

"You are looking for someone who would have been responsible for sending roses here weekly for some time, someone who employed a notorious line of the poet Gertrude Stein?"

"He teaches English."

"Howard Wren?"

"High School English. A private prep school called Gamaliel. He has been there since leaving the University of Chicago. That is where he met Barbara, at the university."

Emtee Dempsey nodded thoughtfully. Kim realized they had not inquired into Wren's background at all, not even after hearing from Victor of Barbara's past friendship with him. But Richard was not through. They had conclusive proof, half a dozen witnesses, that Wren had regularly jogged with Barbara.

"So much for his claim not to have realized she was in the neighborhood and never to have seen her while jogging."

"Have you connected Howard Wren with the stolen van, Richard?"

"We're working on it, Sister. I expect something on that momentarily."

In the wake of all this and after Richard left, Kim wasn't eager to mention the agent's letter. As she had feared, the news brought Emtee Dempsey alive again. She held out her hand for the letter, eyes alight.

"It's two years old, Sister."

Emtee Dempsey smoothed the letter out on her desk and leaned over it. All she lacked was a magnifying glass.

181

"Did the Seltons confirm this was the man who called?"

"No."

Blue eyes regarded Kim through round spectacles. "It was another agent?"

"Mrs. Selton didn't remember the letter and Victor forgot the name. He had made a note for Barbara. I found that when we were looking for the note."

"This is sufficient, Kim. Amazing. Here is a New York literary agent expressing interest in Barbara's writing. If her novel is a good sample of that writing, things are much worse than I realized. Imagine seeing merit or promise in that!" She frowned. "Find out about this man before we confront him."

"Confront him with what?"

"You may be right," the old nun said grimly.

"About what?"

"That Barbara's death will not come as a surprise to him."

Kim fled to the kitchen, unable to witness further the disintegration of a once noble mind. Joyce listened to Kim's account of why the police thought Howard Wren responsible for Barbara's death and to the flimsiness of Emtee Dempsey's alternatives.

"I think I'll have a cigarette."

"I'm tempted to join you."

This shocked Joyce into changing her mind. She slipped her pack of cigarettes back in a drawer, hiding it under discount coupons. Did she think Emtee Dempsey would inspect her kitchen?

"How are you going to check on the man?"

"Adam Pieta? Ask Katherine, I guess."

"Good idea."

They met in the lobby of the Palmer House, their chairs an island of privacy in the midst of constant undistracting activity. Escalators brought people to and from the lobby, there seemed to be an amazing ratio of hotel personnel to guests, there was the muted suggestion of great things afoot on the mezzanine where several conferences were in progress. Katherine scrutinized the letter Kim had brought from Barbara Selton's desk. She shook her head sadly.

"It is a name one is unlikely to forget. Adam Pieta. You will suspect it is a nom de guerre. Not so. It is the name he was born with."

"You know him?"

"Yes. I didn't want to tell you on the phone and arouse hope. The fact is I can imagine this man doing anything, including kill a client."

"You think Barbara became his client?"

"Let me explain."

The explanation was a tale of woe about a journalist friend of Katherine's. "Like all journalists, he dreamed of writing a book. A novel. Unlike most journalists, he actually did so. He was an intelligent young man, very talented, clearly destined for something better than life on a daily paper. He was a man of taste. But why go on? There is some law that such people will produce as fiction something which, were they to pick it up as somebody else's, they would immediately throw down. He was like a new mother. The novel was his baby, he had produced it, he was incapable of critical reflection on it. That would have been like rejection of his very self. For my sins, he gave it to me to read." Katherine took a restorative sip from her gin and tonic.

"Bad?"

Her eyes rolled upward. "Exquisitely awful. Unbelievably bad. For a moment, I hoped it was a hoax, that he knew it was terrible, but no. I dreaded having to give him my verdict. In the event I didn't have to. He had sent a sample to Adam Pieta and the agent phoned to inform him that he had produced a publishable manuscript. I was astounded. And I was very curious about Adam Pieta. The first thing to know about him is that he is unique among literary agents."

Pieta preyed on the yearning to be published that afflicts so many. His ploy was to encourage writers, no matter how bad their effort, and then, when hope had been aroused, to offer to do a detailed analysis of their work. Because he was a busy man, because his overhead on Madison Avenue was what it was, he could not of course do this gratis. A schedule of his fees was enclosed.

"God knows how many fish have taken that bait over the years. My young friend was one of them. Before it was over he had paid out two thousand dollars to Adam Pieta and his novel was no more publishable than when I first saw it. When it was clear that he could squeeze no more money from the man, Pieta submitted the book, got an immediate rejection and washed his hands of the project."

"There's no reason to think Barbara got caught up with Pieta."

"If it was Pieta who telephoned, you may be right. He would not try to bag the same bird twice."

In the course of this conversation, Kim had begun to think that maybe Emtee Dempsey, whatever her motives, had stumbled onto something. It was quite easy to find out.

Katherine telephoned the Adam Pieta agency, identified herself as Barbara Selton, and said she was returning Mr. Pieta's call. The agent came on the line after several minutes delay.

"Barbara Selton?" he said. "You say I called you?"

"That's right."

"Do you live in Chicago?"

"That's right."

"Well, I called a Barbara Dempsey . . ."

And then Katherine remembered Barbara's pen name.

"That's me. I . . . I forgot. You did call?"

"Of course I called. Barbara, I think you have a truly saleable property in *Needy Blood*. It may need a little work. Good Lord, Moby Dick needed a little work. But I think I can place this with a major publisher. I'll demand major promotion, a full tilt effort with the reprint and film rights . . ."

Katherine hung up. She sat for a moment, then recounted to Kim the side of the conversation she had not heard. "Honestly, he could talk me into it. How flattering it must be to a writer to hear a line like that."

"So it did happen."

Katherine agreed. "But what on earth does Sister Mary Teresa think it proves? Surely it has nothing to do with the death of poor Barbara Selton."

"I hope Sister will agree."

7

She certainly listened to every detail with unflagging interest.

"Well, well," she said when Kim was through. "Katherine's description of the man makes his remarks about Barbara's writing intelligible."

"Anyway, he's out."

"Out?"

"Adam Pieta. We can't imagine that he flew to Chicago to kill a potential client. Barbara represented income to him."

"If she fell for his patter."

"Katherine says she herself would have fallen for it. She found him persuasive to a fault."

"Then we can assume he is. Sister Kimberly, I am convinced that this"—she touched the box containing Barbara's manuscript—"is at the bottom of her dreadful death."

"Not if Howard Wren killed her."

"It pains me that I have not yet had the opportunity to speak to that man. Nor am I likely to, now that he is locked up."

"You want me to go talk to him?"

"Splendid idea. Meanwhile, there is something I want Katherine to do."

Richard was considerably less enthused. "He refuses to see a lawyer, why should I let you bother him?"

"He won't see a lawyer?"

"Because he's innocent. Of course they're all innocent until proven guilty. This guy is something. He denies everything. I think if I asked him his name he would deny he is Howard Wren."

"I'm surprised you haven't had a psychiatrist look at him."

"All in good time. Let his lawyer ask for that. When he gets a lawyer."

"I will advise him to get a lawyer."

"Honest Injun?"

"Cross my heart and hope to die."

If she was childish with Emtee Dempsey, she could be childish with her own brother. They at least had been children together.

The sweater Howard Wren wore had Gamaliel emblazoned across the chest.

"I've taught there seventeen years. The headmaster has not come to see me."

It was understandable that Wren's school would be less than elated with the publicity he had brought it. The first stories—Jilted Jogger Arraigned—had not mentioned his place of employment but subsequent stories had emphasized Prep Prof.

"I had difficulty getting to see you myself," Kim said.

The walls of the room seemed excessively featureless, the lights relentlessly bright, bringing out the highlights on Wren's bald skull.

"I had been on my way to see Sister Mary Teresa when they arrested me."

"She sent me here."

He leaned forward, excited. "Why?"

"She thinks the police are on the wrong trail." It seemed cruel to say, particularly because of Wren's reaction.

"Why?"

"It's all pretty circumstantial, isn't it?"

"Of course it is. A and B knew one another, A and B have been seen together. It's absurd."

"Why won't you see a lawyer?"

"I don't have a lawyer."

"We have one. Mr. Benjamin Rush. A wonderful man. Should I speak to him?"

He waved the suggestion away. "Tell me what Sister Mary Teresa thinks."

What else did she have to talk with him about? Kim went into elaborate detail, telling him of the old nun's fascination with Barbara's manuscript, the agent's call.

"Adam Pieta," he repeated, turning his head and looking at her with one eye.

"Katherine Senski says it is his real name. He did call Barbara and did tell her he thought her novel was publishable."

By the time she got around to the roses and Aronstein's truck and a rose is a rose is a rose, his reactions were more moderate.

"She thinks Barbara's death goes back to the roses?"

"There were roses found with the body."

"Three roses?"

"Always three roses. A rose is a rose is a rose."

"Aha. Now that is something the police say nothing about, the roses."

"Leave it to Sister Mary Teresa."

"She is not discouraged?"

"If you knew her you wouldn't ask."

"Barbara admired her."

"Barbara Dempsey," Kim mused. "Not a very effective way to show her admiration."

"I would like to talk with Sister Mary Teresa."

"Mr. Rush could get you out of here. You could come have dinner at Walton Street."

When Richard heard that Wren had asked for a lawyer he was amazed, but when he heard who the lawyer was he had second thoughts.

"Rush! Why would he be interested in a two bit case like this?"

"As a favor."

"Kim, look. This thing is as good as wrapped up. I can say no more now. I don't want Emtee Dempsey making a pest of herself. Believe me, this time she would take a fall. Wren did it. He will be tried and convicted. Bet on it."

"I'll tell Sister."

"Only if it helps. She might take it as a challenge."

When Emtee Dempsey heard this, she held up both hands as if to show they were clean.

"Richard is invited. Tell him I insist that he come."

"Sister, he says they know it was Wren who killed Barbara."

"Of course it was. That is why Richard must come.

Getting the right man is not enough. It is far more important to get the right reason."

It was a thoroughly confused Kim who called her brother and asked him to dinner on Walton Street the following evening.

"I don't know."

Perhaps he was thinking of other occasions when the old nun had pulled a rabbit out of a hat, identifying the murderer, emerging the victor. But she had told Kim not to let Richard know that she agreed that Howard Wren had killed Barbara.

"The Seltons will be here."

"That ought to be fun."

"Richard, it will be all right. Understand. Everything will be all right."

"Is Rush coming?"

"And Katherine Senski."

"I'll be there."

8

Katherine came early, wanting a sneaky pete, a cocktail before the others got theirs.

"She's thrown in the sponge?"

"Maybe, Katherine. But she doesn't act like it. I think we may be in for some surprises."

"But she said Howard Wren is the culprit."

"Yes."

"She wouldn't lie." Katherine seemed to have trouble not letting her remark become a question.

"Sister Mary Teresa would never lie," Kim assured her. Of course her way of telling the truth sometimes resembled lying, but the old nun was always happy to show that there was no question of lying. Could she somehow turn her agreement that Richard was right to think Howard Wren had killed Barbara into a denial?

"What was it that she asked you to do, Katherine?"

"I can't tell."

"Katherine! Now I wish I hadn't told you my news. Emtee Dempsey didn't tell me to let you know."

"Well, she swore me to secrecy."

The doorbell rang then and Kim went to admit Benjamin Rush. Dark suit, green and black striped tie, snow white shirt, their silver-haired lawyer was, as usual, beautifully dressed. Had she ever seen him dressed informally?

"Has my client arrived?"

"Not yet."

"Hmmm. I am always nervous when someone is out on bail. How well do we know this man?"

"Hardly at all."

"I found him completely opaque. Does Sister Mary Teresa think him innocent?"

"No."

"Well, let's pray that he doesn't take a trip."

Emtee Dempsey had gone to the living room from the study and was ensconced in her straight-back brocade chair chatting with Katherine. She greeted Mr. Rush with genuine affection. It occurred to Kim that the three of them were old battlers. Katherine and Mr. Rush had been Emtee Dempsey's allies on the Board of Trustees when she tried to prevent the sale of the college. He had saved this house and the place on Lake Michigan across the Indiana border but the school had been lost. It was disconcerting that the three had been united in a losing cause before.

Victor and his mother came and Kim busied herself making them feel at home which was why Joyce answered the door when Howard Wren arrived and suddenly he was at Kim's elbow. "So this is the legendary house," he said, but his eyes were drawn toward the little old nun. "Will you introduce me?"

Why did she have the feeling that she was bringing adversaries rather than allies together? Howard launched into a eulogy, telling Emtee Dempsey how long ago he had first heard of her from Barbara.

"When she was teaching with us?"

"Yes."

"Was she writing then?"

"She was still at the stage when she talked of writing rather than wrote."

"I have been reading her book reviews."

"Good Lord, how did you find them?"

"It wasn't easy. Do you know them?"

Richard arrived and came immediately to Emtee Dempsey, glancing at Kim as if to ask if he had missed anything. The old nun told him that Howard Wren had just touched on Barbara Selton's book reviews.

"But that will be that for now. Until we have finished dinner there is to be not a single word on the sordid events of the day."

She enforced the rule, an easy task once Joyce's meal was set before them. Veal piccata, asparagus, new potatoes. Dessert was lemon meringue pie, Emtee Dempsey's favorite. The old nun poured coffee, sending the cups around.

"I want to thank you, Victor, for finding the reviews your sister wrote."

"Have you read them?"

"They're marvelous."

"That was her talent, criticism. She took up fiction on a dare."

"Your dare?"

"No."

"Did you ever suggest she become more ambitious?"

"Writing for that shopping guide was a deliberate apprenticeship. Believe me, Barbara had higher goals in mind. I did attempt to prime the pump by sending photocopies of them to an agent."

"That is why Adam Pieta's letter is addressed to her as Barbara Selton?"

He nodded. "She was furious."

Across from Kim, Richard was having difficulty remaining patient. "When are we going to talk about the sordid events of the day?" he asked.

"We have begun to, Richard."

"Look, it's nice that Barbara Selton wanted to be a writer, it's a shame what happened to her, but it is her death that's immediately important."

"And why it happened. You are a writer too, aren't you, Mr. Wren? Or should I say Angelo Stone."

Wren leaned toward her, an odd smile on his face. "Go on."

"Barbara's review of Angelo Stone's experimental novel can only be described as vicious. Don't you agree?"

"Beginning with that quote from Andre Malraux." He tipped back his head and closed his eyes. " 'Is it possible to write fiction now? Every housewife and movie star now writes a novel.' " He opened his eyes. "High school teachers was her addition to the list."

"You published under the name Angelo Stone?"

He nodded.

"*Introit* was your novel."

"Barbara didn't know that when she wrote the review. I made certain she received a copy. It brought us back together again."

"As friends?"

"I expected better of you. The roses?"

Emtee Dempsey sighed. "To catch my attention, and as a clue. Gertrude Stein. The truck stolen from Aronstein's was another."

"But that does not link them to me."

"Stein means stone, doesn't it. What does Angelo Stone mean, the corner stone?"

Wren was beaming now. "You're wonderful! You are everything Barbara said you were. After that review I had to kill her of course, but I wanted to be fair."

"You would reveal yourself in a coded way to me."

Richard wasn't going to sit still for that. "Look, this is all very nice, but let's not forget Wren was arrested and arraigned without any of this stuff."

"Sister Mary Teresa," Benjamin Rush said gently, "you are making my client very difficult to defend."

"Oh, I'll plead guilty now," Wren said. "I gambled and I lost."

"Tell us about it."

Howard Wren was almost euphoric now and he spoke of the bargain Barbara had made. She bet she could write a totally worthless novel and get it published. This was occasioned by a discussion of *Introit*, Barbara not knowing Howard was its author. He winced as he told how his novel had become her point of reference. If that could be published, anything could be. He dared her. She accepted the dare.

"The result was *Needy Blood*. God knows it was awful."

"Terrible," Emtee Dempsey agreed.

"She won when she got the call from New York telling her it was a publishable novel, that it would find a major publisher, receive a major promotion effort."

"And you killed her."

"Yes, but artfully. I made a little bet with myself. She spoke so highly of you, I decided that I would provide you with all you would need to identify me as the murderer. It was not a precipitous act."

"Cold blooded murder," Richard growled.

"Lieutenant, if Barbara were here she would tell you that's a cliche."

"Tell it to the judge."

"I congratulate you, Sister," Wren said, bowing at his hostess. "I have lost twice."

Abruptly he turned, and dashed for the door, bowling Richard over as he left the room. A moment later there was the sound of a tremendous crash. Kim came into the hallway to see Wren sprawled across the floor. Joyce peeked out of the kitchen door.

"He tripped," she said.

But Gleason and O'Connell had come in from their post on the porch, and under Richard's shouted orders took Wren into custody. Richard seemed happy to get away from the house as if he too had lost a bet.

Two hours later, after Mr. Rush had taken Victor and his mother home, Katherine was bidding goodbye, obviously reluctant to leave.

"The beauty of it is that Richard can continue to declare victory."

Emtee Dempsey did not contest this. There was nothing triumphant in her mien. "The poor fellow," she murmured.

"Sister, he is a murderer."

"Yes, yes. But he needn't have been. He thought he lost a bet, but of course he didn't."

"Thinking he could outwit you?"

"No, no, not that. He thought Barbara had won her bet

when she wrote *Needy Blood*. Howard Wren wrongly conceded it was a publishable novel."

After a moment, Katherine said, "Of course. Adam Pieta."

"His judgment was worthless, indeed, if you are right, a deliberate lie."

The irony sank in slowly. But Kim found herself thinking of Barbara. Had she gloated when she heard from Pieta, herself deluded by his judgment, unaware that she was taunting Howard into murdering her?

"Unsurprising, I suppose," Emtee Dempsey concluded. "After all, he apparently regarded 'A rose is a rose is a rose' as a profound observation."

A Sound Investment

When Helen finally inherited the money, it would be the solution to all his difficulties. God knows they had waited long enough. When her father died, George had helped his mother-in-law arrange her affairs, and had realized for the first time how much money Helen would come into.

Helen seemed surprised he was surprised. "Daddy was very successful."

"So was your mother's father."

"I know." She looked at him, then went back to her book.

In the meantime, all the money went to Helen's mother, who, it turned out, had the health of an ox. Fifteen years had gone by since George first learned the size of Helen's eventual inheritance and they had yet to see a nickel of it. Mrs. Wick had open-heart surgery, which strengthened her to bear the other expensive ailments awaiting her. Not that the expense mattered. There was more than enough money for the old lady to be treated for every known disease. But while she survived, Helen had nothing. And things were not going well for George.

The truth was, he had invested unwisely, and with the notion that Helen's money constituted the ultimate collateral. Finally, in desperation, George suggested that Helen ask the lawyers what might be done now.

"What do you mean?" Helen demanded.

"It seems a shame you have to wait."

"George, stop it! Surely you cannot expect me to wish my mother ill."

"Of course not," George said. "But it has to be very tempting for the lawyers, darling. An ailing old woman and all that money. Couldn't—"

"Must we talk of money?"

"I wish we didn't have to."

She sighed. "What's wrong?"

Like a fool, he told her. When he first invested in Subliminal Features, Helen had shaken her head and quoted her father to the effect that a fool and his money are soon parted. (She seemed to think the remark had originated with him.) But George was sure the language lessons encoded on tape along with rock music would sweep the market. The professor whose idea it was was enthusiastic and a colleague, an economist, had prepared a flow chart. Profits were projected to begin before the first year was out. But the only thing Subliminal Features produced was debt. However great an idea, they had thus far been unable to market it effectively. Somewhere in a warehouse were five hundred thousand cassettes containing rock music and encoded lessons in German, Spanish, and French. It was imperative that he get his hands on sixty thousand dollars soon or Subliminal Features would be dead.

"Good money after bad," she said. It was her father speaking.

George went to Briarly, Mrs. Wick's lawyer, and told him his wife was concerned. "Helen doesn't think her mother is gaga, but her mind is not what it was."

"I hadn't noticed."

Briarly was almost as old as Mrs. Wick, which made it difficult to make the point George wanted to make.

"Could Helen be given power of attorney, do you think?"

"I have power of attorney," Briarly said. He worked his mouth, which seemed to have gone dry from lack of use.

"Can nothing be done?"

"In what way?"

George decided to be blunt. "We need money, damn it. Badly. That's why I've come."

"For a loan?"

The old bastard was enjoying this, George realized. He got a grip on himself. "I told her there was no use."

Briarly winced as he got to his feet. Arthritis, probably, George thought. Served the old coot right. "You just tell Helen that she will one day have a great deal of money."

"She already knows that," George said.

"Does she want to borrow money?"

"Against her inheritance, yes."

Briarly looked at George. "Maybe a banker would lend her money on that basis."

George had been to bankers and every one had turned him down, but that was because of what they thought of Subliminal Features. "She wants to borrow from the estate," he said to Briarly.

The old lawyer shook his head. "There is no estate so long as Emilia Wick is alive."

Mrs. Wick was ensconced in the Meadowbrook Manor Communal Residence at an annual cost that, in his present circumstances, made George seethe. But he wouldn't have begrudged the old girl twice that amount if only Helen could have some money now.

Having failed with Helen and with Briarly, not to mention eight bankers, George decided to go to his mother-in-law directly—not something he relished doing. Mrs. Wick had never liked him and made no secret of her view that even now Helen would be better off without him.

She was strapped into a wheelchair and had her denture in one hand and the remote control of her TV in the other. The sight of her son-in-law brought a frown rather than a smile. She motioned him to a chair, on which was a bedpan fastidiously covered with a cloth. He put the pan on the floor somewhat noisily and Mrs. Wick turned the sound of the television several punishing decibels higher.

The soap opera lasted an hour and was followed by another. George sat through both, pretending interest—not that Emilia noticed or cared—rehearsing what he would say to her. Briarly was right—she was not gaga. Her mind was alert and sharp. If she wanted to settle an amount of money on her daughter now, her lawyer would have no choice but to follow her wishes.

A game show came on and Mrs. Wick snickered with pleasure. "I want to talk with you," George said earnestly and she did not shush him as she had before. "It's about Helen." Mrs. Wick fixed a birdlike eye on him. "She made a bad investment and is rather deeply in debt."

"Her, too?"

"What do you mean?"

"She told me you lost a bundle of money on some stupid scheme."

"Did she ask you for money?"

The denture she had put back in her mouth during the second soap opera made her smile seem almost sinister. "It wouldn't matter if she did. It was only after my father died that I received any of his money."

His mother-in-law's eyes were fixed on him and he had the unsettling feeling she could read his thoughts. He smiled reassuringly, wondering how physically strong she really was. If only he could think of some way to ease her into the next world painlessly, he was sure Helen would not find the loss irreparable. After all, she rarely visited her mother now. All these aging people depressed her too much.

George looked at the pillow on his mother-in-law's bed and imagined holding it over her face while she slipped into eternity, thinking of it as a means of reunion with her husband, her parents, all her departed friends. Looked at in that way, it seemed a favor he might do her.

A nurse came and put Emilia to bed and George got up to go.

"Could you get her earphones for that set?" the nurse asked him in the hallway. "She won't turn it down."

George stared at her. She might have been a co-conspirator. "I'll bring a set tomorrow," he said.

He bought a headset on his way home and that night worked on it at his workbench in the basement. The idea was simple—what made it difficult was making what he intended to happen look like an accident. The headset was an import, probably assembled on boats in the Hong Kong harbor. An uncovered wire pressed to the ear. The current at Meadowbrook would be more than sufficient. A little more work and he was sure they would lock onto her head, explaining why he had been unable to remove them.

"That's very nice of you, George," Helen said the next morning.

He lifted his shoulders humorously. "I might be old myself someday."

At Meadowbrook, he showed the nurse at the reception desk what he had brought for Mrs. Wick.

"Thank God."

Emilia listened to his explanation and looked at the

headset warily. "Show me how it works, George."

"Of course." Later he would use the attachment in his pocket to connect the headset to a wall socket. Now he plugged it into the television and put it carefully on his head. It was like shutting out the world. Too late, he remembered what he had done. The headset locked in place. Emilia smiled at him as if from the other side of glass and then her hand moved on the remote control. The sound struck his ears like cymbals slamming together, then rose higher, his mind seeming to soar with the sound to new pinnacles of pain and madness. He tried to tear the set off, but it only gripped his head more securely while an arthritic finger pushed the volume higher and higher.

Eventually he was given a room on the next floor, where he could be watched around the clock. He was young for Meadowbrook, but seemed somehow older, because his mind was gone.

And though his hearing was impaired—maybe because it was—he developed a fondness for the rock music his wife brought him, and a night nurse swore she had heard him speaking German in his sleep.

The Visitor

Wanda pulled the door open furiously, expecting to see Leonard there, back before he left for work for a final shot about the bill she had run up consulting psychic advisers.

"Do you meditate, madam?"

"Meditate!"

Prepared to give as good as she got from Leonard in what promised to be an epic quarrel, one of those that stretched over a week, Wanda was startled by the tall man with the shaven head whose eyes seemed to look inward as much as outward at her.

"So few people do. How old are you?"

"That's none of your business." Her hand gripped the door but she found herself unable to slam it in his face. "You know your age, that's what's important. How many years do you suppose you have left?"

He lifted his face, as if expecting an answer from on high. He lowered his eyes to her once more.

"Madam, would you step outside, please?"

"I'm not dressed."

"That is why you are reluctant to ask me in. We must talk."

It was a challenge. Of course she would ask him in. It wasn't as if she were indecent, for pete's sake. She wore a wrapper over her nightgown, and on her feet were the silly pink slippers with toes the shape of bunny heads that Leonard had bought her during one of the lulls in their long-term argument.

"My name is Alexander," he said. He wore a business suit, light grey, with a purple shirt buttoned at the neck. The chain with the odd pendant might have been his necktie. He drifted into the living room and looked mournfully around.

"What's wrong?"

"There is no *you* here."

"Are you selling something?"

"Whatever I have is not mine to own. It is yours as much as mine." He sat, but as one sits who may leave at any minute. Suddenly she wanted him to stay. She had the sense that this man, Alexander, was someone to whom she could talk, someone who would understand her. A bell sounded insistently from the back of the house and Wanda made an impatient noise.

"Ah," Alexander said, holding it as if it were a note and he about to chant.

"That's Mattie. My mother-in-law."

"And she summons you."

"Will you excuse me a minute?"

"I will come with you."

And he did, down the hallway to the kitchen and through the breezeway to the apartment they had made for Mattie in what had once been the garage. The kitchen was a mess, but at this hour of the day what could you expect? Wanda wanted Alexander to see what her life was like, what she had to put up with.

Mattie was propped up in the La-Z-Boy chair she preferred to her bed, forever readjusting it in search of some angle of restfulness that would make life tolerable. Her hair stood on her scalp as if she had her finger in the light socket. She cocked her head and looked at Alexander.

"Who are you?"

"You are in the vestibule of the beyond, Martha. This is no time to ask childish questions. How is your soul?"

The old woman looked up at him pop-eyed and then, incredibly, burst into tears. Her scrawny veined hand reached for him, clawing at the air, until he took it, enveloping hers in his own two large hands. He turned to Wanda.

"Leave us alone."

Wanda turned and went back through the breezeway to the kitchen, where she began to clean up. She felt excitement. Something very important was happening. For five years, Wanda had been little more than her mother-in-law's keeper, waiting on her hand and foot, on edge all day, forever expecting that damned bell to ring. Whenever she hid the bell, the old woman would begin to whimper, a penetrating sound that crept through the house and found her no matter where she hid from it.

"Wanda, in a little while, it will all be ours."

That was Leonard's argument. They had moved in here with his mother, selling their house at a loss, but what the hell, they were through paying rent or mortgage installments. Wanda had calculated that they had sunk more money into Mattie's house than they would have paid staying in their own over that five-year period. Leonard did not want to bill his mother for improvements—the new drive, fencing along the back of the yard, the roof, and the redesign of the garage that was meant to give them a little breathing space from Mattie.

"You'll have your privacy this way, Mom."

"Why don't you just put me out with the trash?"

"Stop talking like that."

"This is a garage."

"Not anymore."

Leonard actually suggested that they move into the remodeled garage and let the old woman have the rest of the house.

"Over my dead body."

"You sound like her."

"I'm going to look like her before . . ."

"Before what?"

"I don't want to talk about it."

"You want her dead, don't you? Well, say it: I wish Martha Bertle were dead."

"Don't you?"

That shut him up. Wasn't he something, trying to make her feel guilty? This idea had been a conspiracy from the beginning. They would ingratiate themselves with Mattie. His sister in Seattle sent a Christmas card that wasn't even signed, just Mr. and Mrs. Patrick Pringle, printed. Once the legend had been from Pringle Pharmacy. Laura obviously considered her mother already dead and gone. If Mattie could be made to realize that the only one who cared for her was Leonard, and Wanda, of course, well, then . . .

"We get this house?"

"That's not the half of it."

"How do you know?"

"You've seen the bankbook."

"Where would I see her bankbook?"

"It doesn't matter. She doesn't trust banks. Except insofar as they rent safe-deposit boxes."

"Does she have a safe-deposit box?"

Leonard adopted a sly smile and nodded slowly. It turned

out he had never seen what was in it. He got angry when she suggested it was empty. That was the first quarrel that lasted more than two days. When the clouds cleared and the sun shone once more, Leonard said they had to get a look into that safety-deposit box.

After a month of discreet searching in the garage apartment, Wanda found the little envelope with the key to the safety-deposit box. Like a fool, she let Leonard talk her into going down to the bank and asking to open the box.

"Don't let on you're not the right Mrs. Bertle."

So Wanda showed the young man the key and he asked her to sign a little slip. That was when she sensed this wasn't going to work. He took the slip and riffled through a card index from which eventually he plucked a card. He laid her slip alongside the card. He frowned.

"You're Mrs. Bertle?"

"That's right."

"The signatures don't match."

"That's my mother-in-law's."

"This is her safety-deposit box?"

"She asked me to get something for her." Wanda leaned forward. "She's quite helpless now."

This posed a problem. The young man rose and crossed the floor as if he had a gun in his back and consulted with a woman whose hair was an artful mess. Her head began to sway negatively as she listened. The two came to where Wanda was sitting.

The woman nodded to the young man, who narrated what had happened to this point in time.

"Our Mrs. Bertle is your mother-in-law, Mrs. Bertle?" the woman asked.

"Yes."

"And you want to open her safety-deposit box?" She said

this as if she were recounting an attempt at sacrilege. "The bank enters into the most solemn of arrangements with the holders of safety-deposit boxes, Mrs. Bertle."

She preached on, unctuously. Wanda felt as if she were the blackest of sinners.

"You must obtain power of attorney. Then and only then can we let you see Mrs. Bertle's box."

This and the many other annoying, aggravating, infuriating, humiliating episodes that had characterized her life since she and Leonard had moved in with Mattie went past Wanda's mind as she tidied up the kitchen. She realized that Alexander was standing in the doorway. When their eyes met she was certain he knew every secret of her life, that he had been inside her mind and memory while she had reviewed her dreadful life with Mattie.

"She will soon be dead," Alexander said.

"Mattie?"

He nodded, his eyes reading her soul.

"But she's strong as a horse."

"You are going to speed her on her way."

Trying to laugh it off did not work, not with his hypnotic eyes on her. He suggested that they return to the living room. There he spoke in a soft musical voice about the swiftness with which life passes, how the vast majority of human beings are so caught up in the trivia of everyday tasks that they never seriously ask themselves the only important question. He fell silent.

"What is the question?"

He nodded, as if they were already in agreement. "What does it all mean?"

He elaborated. Moments become minutes which become hours, and the hours turn into days, the earth spins clockwise round the sun, its orbit altering into seasons, and the years follow one another, but from a cosmic perspective, earthly millennia are insignificant. Think of the light year.

Wanda realized she hadn't thought of much of anything since she quit work to stay home with Mattie, and before that what she had thought about was her work. College? A four-year blur. Listening to Alexander, Wanda felt her mind stir from slumber and begin to operate in uncustomary but pleasant ways. The thought emerged that it was a very bad waste of the few winks of time she had on earth to be fretting over Mattie.

"She too longs for this to be over."

"Did you talk with her about it?"

"Of course."

"What am I supposed to do?"

It was laughably simple. Alexander knew of the sealed can in the basement containing the stuff Leonard put on his roses. She felt that Alexander knew everything. Bring the container upstairs, add a spoonful to the tea she made for Mattie, sit with her while she drank it, making her last moments pleasant. That was all there was to it.

"She doesn't want to do it herself?"

"Of course she wants to, but when is the last time she made the tea?"

At any other time that question could have started her on a litany of complaints. There was no physical reason for Mattie to sit atrophying in her chair day and night. It was sheer stubborn meanness. But Alexander was right. She was too mean even to poison herself. She would want Wanda to do it.

"I'll talk it over with Leonard tonight."

Alexander shook his head. "No. She doesn't want him to know. Besides, by tonight it will all be over."

"She wants me to do it today?"

"She longs for it."

"Talk to me some more."

"I have talked enough. Now you must meditate."

And it was over. He rose, went to the door, and was outside before she could move. When she looked down the drive, there was no sign of him. On the other side of the street, a car moved off.

Wanda went back to the living room, sat, and shut her eyes, intent on meditating. But the image of the sealed can in the basement formed in her mind and wouldn't go away. First she would bring it upstairs. She put it on the kitchen counter and sat on a stool. Her mind refused to concentrate on anything. She went back to see how Mattie was doing.

Her chair was upright, her hair brushed; she looked neat as a pin. "I liked him."

"Alexander?"

"He understands the situation here."

"I've needed someone to talk with."

"So have I."

"You're no good at it, talk."

"I'm sorry."

"This whole thing was a mistake, I knew that from the beginning," Mattie sighed. "Well, it is time I got out of it."

She put back her head and closed her eyes. How happy she looked, and expectant. Wanda felt almost holy at the thought that she would help Mattie go on to a better place. Alexander spoke of it as far out beyond the galaxies, a place toward which one moved with incredible swiftness, yet it required an eternity to get there.

"Where the big bang took place," he whispered.

"Did he speak to you of the big bang?" Wanda asked the old woman.

But Mattie had drifted off, the sweetest smile on her dry thin lips.

Wanda thought of telephoning Leonard, to give him some indication of what his mother had decided, but Alexander's warning that she not tell him kept her from the phone. It was Leonard who called her.

"I'm sorry," he said, without preamble.

"Me too."

"I know how hard it is on you to live the way we do."

"It's not forever."

"That's right. We have to remember that."

"Your mother has been such an angel today."

"Angel?"

And soon she would be among the angels, hair brushed, bright-eyed, ready for that long long journey toward the place where the big bang had taken place.

Leonard said he would be late and she urged him to come as soon as he could. What lay before her was vague but inevitable.

She took a sandwich in to Mattie at noon.

"I hate chicken salad."

"That's tuna."

"Did you make tea?"

"We'll have that later. The two of us."

"I want it now."

Well, she ought to have it when she wanted it. Wanda leaned toward the old woman, seeking in her expression some sign of the secret they shared, but Mattie turned away.

"You're blocking the sun."

How easy it was to tolerate the cranky old woman now. It would all be over soon. She made her a simple cup of tea to have with her sandwich. She and Mattie would have high tea at the usual time. It seemed wrong to break the routine on this last day.

Mattie sipped the tea suspiciously and wrinkled her

nose. "It always tastes the same."

It was the only hint she gave of what they were going to do. Had she expected her luncheon tea to contain the fatal dose? She napped again after Wanda took away her tray. Wanda lay down for her nap but she could not sleep. She went back in with Mattie and sat there, watching the old woman sleep, imagining that she had already made tea in the way Alexander had told her the old woman wanted and Mattie had already begun her long astral journey to the beginning of it all.

"What are you doing here?"

Wanda snapped awake at the angry sound of Mattie's voice. It was nearly three o'clock.

"I fell asleep."

"I could see that."

Anger flared up in Wanda until she remembered. While she slept she had dreamed of Alexander, of his commanding presence, and of his soothing voice coming musically to her out of infinite space and time. She had read of people who claimed to have visions, heavenly visitations, who had been snatched up in alien spacecraft and taken on strange flights. Such stories no longer seemed incredible. If she had to describe Alexander, it would be difficult to make him sound like an earth person. Of course it was Mattie he had come for, not her. She was merely the instrument of the plan Alexander had drawn forth from deep inside Mattie's soul. She was ready to go now and she wanted a little help to put her on her way.

"I'm hungry."

"It hasn't been two hours since we had lunch."

"Let's have our tea."

"Be patient, Mattie. We'll have it at four, as we always do."

"I can't wait till four."

"Yes, you can."

They both could. Wanda went solemnly into the main house, leaving Mattie alone with her thoughts. The bell jangled as it usually did, but Wanda ignored it, not out of anger, as she might have before, but wanting Mattie to think of what lay ahead. To meditate. They could talk when it came time for tea.

In the kitchen she took a measuring cup and put into it two tablespoonfuls of the stuff from the can she had brought up from the basement. The odor when she pried open the lid was the odor of earth, of death, of a tomb sealed for centuries but opened now. She put the measuring cup by the teakettle and pressed the lid down tight on the can. She returned it to its place on the basement shelf. It was 3:45 when she came up to the kitchen again.

She put on the water and went into the breezeway and strained her ear. Mattie was talking to herself. It seemed almost as good as meditation.

She put tea in the pot and then poured the contents of the measuring cup in as well. The whistle on the kettle began its shrill sound and she took it from the fire. The sound of Mattie's voice died away. She would know that tea was on its way.

Wanda added the boiling water to the pot, replaced the top, and slipped a cozy over it. She would let it steep a few minutes before taking it in. The tea cart was one Mattie had had for years and it meant much to her to have her tea rolled in to her on it. Wanda made little sandwiches and petits fours and then put the teapot on the cart.

"Tea time," she sang out, and started toward the garage apartment.

She rolled the cart up next to Mattie's chair, in case she wanted to pour. But the old woman sat with folded hands, an expectant look on her face as she surveyed the goodies on the cart. Wanda poured a cup and handed it to her mother-in-law. It was a solemn moment. Mattie waited while she added milk and sugar, she liked lots of sugar, then stirred vigorously. How eager she looked.

Wanda poured another cup and took a chair. Mattie sipped, pursed her lips against the heat, then sipped again. She took a sandwich from the cart and nibbled delicately on it, then drank more tea.

"Mmmmmm," she said.

She drank it down and held up her cup for more. Wanda poured again. Mattie would want a third cup, she always did, and usually Wanda discouraged it since it meant several trips to the bathroom, but today she gladly poured the third cup.

And waited. She brought her own cup to her lips, then stopped. Dear God, she was not ready for any trip through the stars, not yet, not when finally her long agony was coming to an end. She and Leonard would be alone, the cause of their quarrels would be gone, the future would lie bright ahead of them again.

Mattie's grip on her cup loosened and it rolled down her lap and onto the floor. The old woman's head had snapped back and she was gasping for air. Wanda had not been prepared for this. She had expected Mattie simply to drift into sleep. But instead the old woman fought against going, scratching at her throat, fixing Wanda with her bright angry eyes until her eyelids fluttered, her eyes rolled upward, and she slumped forward.

Wanda straightened the old woman in her chair and tried to smooth away the awful expression on her face. The doorbell rang.

She stood, feeling panic at first, and then, remembering Alexander's visit earlier, hurried through the house to the front door, pulling it open with a great smile.

"Nine-one-one," a man said, pushing past her. He was followed by another. "Where is she?"

"Who?"

"The woman who's been poisoned."

She managed to point and they sped through the house. She followed. They reached the breezeway and went right on, as if they knew now where they were going. Wanda couldn't watch while they worked over Mattie. Before she left, she saw one of the paramedics shrug at the other. She was seated at the kitchen table when they came in.

"She's dead."

"I know."

"We came as quickly as we could."

"Who called you? Alexander?"

"I think it was your husband."

"My husband."

They checked and it was true, Leonard had phoned 911 to report that his mother had just been given poison and would they get over there as quickly as they could.

Given poison. That phrase was the beginning of her realization that something was wrong. She tried to tell the paramedics about Alexander and how he had talked to Mattie, but their eyes kept moving away. More police arrived. She asked them to call Leonard and the phone was pushed toward her. Leonard was not in his office.

He had said he would be late tonight. He was not yet home when a detective advised her to call a lawyer. "My husband is my lawyer."

"You'll want someone else, ma'am. After all, he made the call."

Leonard had not come home when she was taken downtown and he did not come to see her. The lawyer she eventually got was named Sawyer. He just looked at her when she told him about Alexander but later, as the trial approached, he wanted to hear all about it.

"That's our only defense," he said. "Nobody will believe it."

"That's the idea."

Leonard still had not come to see her. How could she complain? After all, she was accused of killing his mother. In the end, she pleaded guilty by reason of insanity. She had never been so humiliated in her life. When she stood for sentencing, she turned and looked at the few curious people in the courtroom. Leonard was there. He was talking to the man beside him, a tall man with a crew cut. And then Leonard looked toward her and their eyes met. But it was the face of the man beside him Wanda saw, the great staring eyes, the look of serenity.

"Alexander!" she screamed. "There he is."

She was wrestled into her chair by the matron but she continued to call out. They had to listen. The man who was responsible was there in the courtroom with her husband. Two more matrons were required to remove her from the courtroom. Sawyer came to tell her what her sentence was.

"As soon as the doctors say you're okay, you go free."

She nodded. In the interim since being removed from the courtroom, she had begun to understand.

"A piece of advice," Sawyer said. "Forget about Alexander. As long as you talk about him, they're going to keep you locked up."